DAY OF THE MOON

Other *Mystery Scene* books available from Carroll & Graf:

Beyond the Grave
by Marcia Muller and Bill Pronzini

Buyer Beware
by John Lutz

Dead Pigeon
by William Campbell Gault

Dead Run
by Bill Pronzini

In the Heat of the Night
by John Ball

The Jade Figurine
by Bill Pronzini

The Lighthouse
by Marcia Muller and Bill Pronzini

Touch of Evil
by Whit Masterson

Tough Tender
by Max Allan Collins

DAY OF THE MOON

BILL PRONZINI & JEFFREY WALLMANN

Carroll & Graf Publishers, Inc.
New York

Copyright © 1983 by Bill Pronzini and Jeffrey Wallmann

All rights reserved

Published by arrangement with the authors.

First Published by Robert Hale, London.

First Carroll & Graf edition 1993.

Carroll & Graf Publishers, Inc.
260 Fifth Avenue
New York, NY 10001

ISBN: 0-88184-976-6

Manufactured in the United States of America

ONE

Flagg tripped the lock with a piece of celluloid from his coat pocket, shoved open the door and went into the room with the .38 Special held easily in his right hand.

"Lie still," he said, "the both of you."

The thin, pale young man and the buxom redhead were wrapped in each other's arms in the middle of the iron frame bed. They remained that way and Flagg thought that they looked like a very good imitation of a sculpure by Rodin. He shut the door, went over to stand by the wall next to the window.

"Get up, Karensky," he said.

Pete Karensky pushed the redhead away and gained his feet. He stood awkwardly, his narrow shoulders trembling. There was sweat on his forehead. The redhead folded a dingy, threadbare sheet around herself and lay there looking scared.

"What the hell?" Karensky said in a reedy, tremulous voice. "Who're you? You're not a cop."

"No," Flagg said, "I'm not."

"Then what do you want?"

"Just the money."

"What money?"

"One hundred and eleven thousand dollars," Flagg said patiently. "The take from the Herald Armored Car heist this morning."

Karensky's face became even paler. "I don't know anything about that. How would I know anything about that?"

"Because you were the inside man," Flagg said. "Somebody had to plant that gas package in the armored car's heater duct. Somebody who knew how to rig a solenoid so it could be set off by a radio signal. A mechanic, Karensky. A mechanic with access to the armored car. A Herald mechanic. You, Karensky. You're the boy."

Karensky was trembling violently now and his face had the color and consistency of tainted buttermilk. Looking at him, Flagg wondered how a pro like Gino Trenotti could have put his trust in such a jellyfish. But in order to pull the job off, Trenotti had needed an inside man and he must have figured that it was worth the risk. He'd figured wrong.

Flagg said, "Where's the money?"

"Listen," Karensky said. "Listen, what makes you think I know where the money is? I don't know anything about it."

"You're only making it harder on yourself."

"You think I killed him, don't you?" Karensky said. His voice had risen to a shrill falsetto. "You really think I shot this guy, this Trenotti, and took the money for myself."

Flagg watched him.

"I don't care how it looks!" Karensky said. "I didn't kill him! I couldn't kill a man! I couldn't kill anybody!"

"No? Trenotti's dead."

"I tell you, I don't know nothing about it!"

"Then why'd you run?"

"I was scared," Karensky said. "It . . . It just got to me after a while. I got sick at the garage this morning and they sent me home. I didn't want to leave, because this Trenotti told me to stay put on the job, but they wouldn't let me stay. They said if I was sick, I had to go home. What could I do? I had to go, and I was sitting in my apartment with Sharon when I heard about the hold-up on the radio.'

"Sure," Flagg said.

"I was, I swear I was! It all came over the radio, about Trenotti being found with a bullet in his throat, right there beside the armored car, and the money being gone and the solenoid package still in the heater. I knew they'd tie it to me, so I packed some things and we left. We figured to get down to Mexico maybe, someplace where we couldn't be found."

The fear was naked on Karensky's sallow face and the more Flagg studied him, the less he liked Karensky for the hit. It took courage to doublecross a man like Trenotti, a tough ex-con who'd been in the heist business for twenty years; and it took cold nerve to put a bullet into a man's throat while he was looking at you.

"Listen," Karensky said, spreading his hands in an almost feminine gesture of helplessness. "If I'd killed Trenotti, wouldn't I have pulled that solenoid package from the heater? Wouldn't I? That's the thing that wraps it up for the cops, that package. Without it, they don't know how the gas got into the armored car to knock out the guards and they can't say for sure that there was an inside man. Isn't that right?"

"Maybe," Flagg said. He glanced from Karensky to the redhead huddled under the bedsheet. "Are you Sharon?"

She nodded, moistening her lips and staring at him out of huge green eyes. She wasn't bad-looking, Flagg thought, but she couldn't have had much in the way of intelligence to have taken up with a jerk like Karensky.

Flagg asked her: "Where were you at eleven this morning?"

"With Pete."

"Where?"

"At his place."

"What time did you leave?"

"When we heard the news about the hold-up."

Flagg studied her. She had one of those faces that were as easy to read as a first-grade primer. He didn't think her answers had been rehearsed dialogue. He would have been able to tell by her eyes and expression if they had been.

"All right," Flagg said. He stared away from the wall, moving toward the door.

"What're you going to do now?"

Flagg opened the door and glanced out into the hallway. Then he stepped into the doorway with his left hand on the knob and his right holding the .38 at waist level.

"If I were you, Karensky," he said, "I'd stay right where you are. I wouldn't try running any farther. I found you this time without any trouble at all, and I can find you again, here or in Mexico or anywhere else. The easier you make it for me to reach you if I want you, the better it'll be."

"But the cops—"

"Take your choice," Flagg said, and stepped into the hallway, slamming the door behind him. He strode toward the stairs at the far end of the corridor, slipping his .38 Special into his clamshell semi-shoulder holster, buttoning his sport jacket at the waist.

The stairs creaked. The building, old and wooden, smelling of dryrot and urine, was located in a tenement district of a city two hundred miles south of San Francisco. It reminded Flagg of the Upper West Side ratholes in New York City where he had lived as a boy. But he felt no bitterness because of it; that had been a long time ago, in another time and another world, and he had profited by it the same way you profited by all your experiences—as long as you survived them.

He hesitated in the dark foyer of the building for a moment, listening and peering into the cloudy night. A small neon sign above the entrance buzzed to itself; the H and O of HOTEL flickered, casting a pale spotlight on the cracked sidewalk in front of him.

Flagg crossed the street to his nondescript Chevrolet sedan, parked facing the entrance to Highway 101 a block away. The car was unlocked on the driver's side and latched only by its safety catch, just as he had left it. He drove north, toward San Francisco.

Traffic was light. He made good time through Paso Robles, King City and Salinas, but got bogged down some when he passed through Gilroy and Morgan Hill, because of the long stretch of well-lit, suburban development. Just before San Jose, he ran into a road gang repaving a quarter-mile section. The blinking barricades and reflector cones, which had been set up to block off one lane, reminded him of the way Trenotti had pulled off the Herald Armored Car heist.

Gino Trenotti had always been one to take advantage of any given situation and, when he had come upon the detour on River Valley Road in the East Bay, it hadn't taken him long to dream up a way to use it. River Valley Road ran from San Ramon to Martinez, two bedroom communities a bit east of Oakland, but the road itself had fallen into disuse after the straighter, four-lane Route 506 had been built. It was still the only way to Lamont Laboratories, however, and Lamont was one of those sweet targets a good heist man like Trenotti kept filed in the back of his mind.

Lamont Laboratories was typical of the many government-contract, aerospace companies in the area, yet differed from the others in that it was controlled by a brilliant but eccentric old physicist—Caspar Lamont —who still believed cash was better than cheques. High-salaried engineers and a blue-collar force of assemblers commanded a twice-monthly payroll of over seventy-five thousand dollars, and Christmas bonuses jacked that up to a hundred grand, all in cash and all carried by Herald.

Most businessmen would have blanched at the notion of such a prime temptation, but you can't argue with success. And Old Man Lamont had been successful, or just plain damn fool lucky, right up until the time Trenotti chanced across the detour. It was located just before the spot where a winter-swollen Ridge River had washed out an old concrete bridge. Narrow and often merely a rutted trail, the detour wandered through the hills for some six miles, before it angled back to River Valley Road on the other side of the fallen bridge.

Trenotti had discovered the detour in early November, Flagg knew, only three months after he had been released on parole from Oregon State Prison, where he had spent most of five years for burglary. Trenotti was a Pacific Northwest boy, though he had not been above working in California if the opportunity was right; and he had prided himself on never having used a gun on a job. But armored cars are hard to take without one, so Trenotti had decided to risk an armed robbery charge in order to get a crack at this fat one, hoping to pull it off and be back in Oregon before his parole violation could be noticed. He had lost the gamble.

Finding the detour had been accidental; Trenotti had happened on it while tracking down an old lover of his, a lady he never did manage to locate. His next visits had been purposeful. He had watched two deliveries before he made any move, taking his time setting up the heist, making his arrangements for bankrolling and protection. The hardest part of the job had to have been uncovering the weak link in the Herald garage, Flagg thought as he drove. Trenotti had to have canvassed each employee carefully before approaching any of them. If he had dropped a hint to the wrong one, the whole thing would have been queered.

After Trenotti had settled on Karensky, though, and his pitch had been accepted, then the rest would have been duck soup: The gas package rigged in the heater duct; the wait on an off-road until the armored car passed on the detour; the signal from a model-aeroplane control to trigger the release of the gas; the pickup of the car with the tow-truck, after the driver and the two guards had fallen unconscious and the car had drifted off the road . . .

Flagg cut off 101 onto the Nimitz Freeway. The very first rays of dawn made the hills on his right glow slightly, as if they were being heated by a torch. Like the acetylene outfit Trenotti had used to get into the armored car, Flagg thought, after he had towed it onto the deserted and screened off-road.

According to his plan, Trenotti would have had sufficient time to torch the armored car's rear-door lock, fill his waiting Dodge Sportsman van with the sacks of money, remove the gas package and drive away before anyone at Lamont could become suspicious. It would have been simple and sweet, with nobody hurt, the trademark of a Trenotti hit. Except that something had happened to screw it up.

Precisely what had happened was still open to question. All that was known so far was that when the driver and guards had regained consciousness, they had seen the tow-truck and the van. And they had seen Trenotti lying beside the van's open doors, a bullet lodged in his windpipe and blood soaking into the ground around him from where the bullet had torn through his jugular vein. But they had not seen the money. Since then, nobody had seen any trace of the money. Nobody, that is, except the bastard who had murdered Trenotti for it.

Of course the gas package, which the Highway Patrol investigators soon found in the heater duct, led straight back to the Herald garage. With a little checking, it led from there straight to Karensky, who by then had all but confessed his guilt by skipping town.

And of course Flagg had figured the killing the same way the police surely had: No matter if Trenotti had been shot on purpose, in panic, or during a struggle, he must have been shot by Karensky. After all, Karensky was the inside man, the only one who knew the plan and could be in a position to stage a double-cross.

Karensky fit the crime perfectly. But now, having caught up and talked with him, Flagg no longer thought so. Call it intuition, call it experience, he just didn't like Karensky for it at all.

Problem was, that left Flagg with nobody else.

And he liked that a hell of a lot less.

TWO

Flagg turned off the Nimitz and stopped at a Union service station for gas. While the tank was being filled, he walked to where a phone booth stood at the curb of the station's lot—and called Churlak at his private home number in San Francisco.

"Flagg," he said when Churlak answered. "I'm back."

"With the money?"

"No. Karensky's not our boy."

"Christ. Are you sure?"

"I'm satisfied till something proves different."

"Well, what are your plans now?"

"To forget the police theory and go back and start from scratch, the way I should've done in the first place." Flagg paused to rub his eyes and cheeks with his left hand, feeling weary and irritable. "I'd like to know what Trenotti did. Will you check it for me?"

"What do you mean, what he did?—"

"I mean he was on parole, right? Oregon wouldn't have let him out if he hadn't had a job lined up, a legit job; I want to know what it was. There might be a connection there, somehow."

"I doubt it. Trenotti was a clam."

"Chalk it up to my curiosity, then."

"All right, give me a couple of hours. I'll be in my office; you can reach me there."

Flagg hung up and returned to his car. He paid the gas bill with cash, then swung onto Highway 50 to San Ramon. The police had no way of telling whether there were other accomplices besides Karensky involved, but Flagg would have been surprised if there were. Churlak was right; Trenotti was too much of a pro to make a slip of the tongue either here or up in Oregon, and though Karensky might have, Flagg didn't think Trenotti would have divulged anything more than necessary. So whatever Trenotti's legitimate employment had been, it was a long shot at best, and Flagg didn't figure it would turn out to be an important lead, any more than Churlak did.

Yet the only other explanation, at least on the surface, was that some stranger had happened along at an opportune moment and had taken advantage of the circumstances. Flagg had an even harder time swallowing that sort of coincidence; it was too foreign for his well-ordered mind. He was convinced there was more to it than that. He felt it. Something had been overlooked, which was why he had asked Churlak about Trenotti's work; if nothing else, Flagg was thorough.

Just on the other side of San Ramon, after the exit for 560, Flagg slowed and turned off onto River Valley Road. Three miles later came the detour, angling toward the east. A mile more and Flagg spotted the off-road, hardly more than a hiker's path. Right past it were skid marks and a crumpled section of fencing to mark the point where the armored car had rolled into the shoulder ditch.

Flagg turned onto the off-road. Thick scrub-brush scraped at his car's sides and underbelly and he was forced to reduce his speed to a crawl. He came around a stiff bend, onto a flat grassy knoll that was hidden from the detour by a heavy stand of eucalyptus.

He parked his car just off the trail and stepped out into the chill, whistling wind that fanned across the knoll. It was full dawn now and the sun was a filtered yellow disc seen through a bank of haze to the east. Flagg shrugged into his overcoat and buttoned it up to his throat, then began looking carefully around.

There were the tracks in the soft earth made by the armored car, and by the tow-truck and Dodge van, and by the multitude of official vehicles which had been there during the subsequent investigation. Footprints obliterated some of the tracks. There were other signs of the search that had been conducted in the area: broken branches on surrounding shrubs, tufts of earth pulled or kicked loose, cigarette and cigar butts and candy wrappers strewn about.

Flagg stepped away from his car and went toward the stand of eucalyptus, still trying to puzzle things through. One odd fact that kept bothering him was that the pistol belonging to the Herald driver had had one shot fired from it. The driver had told the police he'd awakened with it in his hand, though he could not recall firing it or even drawing it. Assuming that was true, it followed the killer must have put it there — which made no sense to Flagg, because the driver's gun was not the murder weapon. The same calibre, yes, but the barrel striations on the bullet taken from Trenotti had not matched those on the bullets test-fired from the driver's gun.

Briefly Flagg considered that perhaps the driver had come out of the gas earlier than expected and had killed Trenotti with another gun, maybe a spare kept in the armored-car cab for emergencies. But that didn't wash either. If the driver was the killer, why would he have fired a bullet from his own revolver? And then there was the gas: Flagg knew the type Trenotti had used, and you just didn't wake up with full faculties a few minutes after exposure to it.

No, it had to've been somebody else, somebody chancing upon Trenotti looting the armored car, somebody coincidentally carrying the same make and calibre of service revolver as the driver's.

Flagg shook his head. Originally he had assumed his task would be simple, his only real problem being to locate Karensky and the money before the cops did. But now, having discounted Karensky, he was left with the matter blown apart, and all this speculation was leading nowhere. To hell with it. He didn't care for the idea of prowling around up here at eight o'clock in the morning—the police had been over this stretch time and again the day before, and they were pretty damn good—but he had no place else to start now that he had ruled out Karensky.

He searched all the eucalyptus grove and the immediate area surrounding the knoll. He found nothing unusual, nothing the local cops and Highway Patrol might have overlooked. It wasn't any use; he was just wasting his time.

He was at the bottom of the hill now, on the other side of the knoll near the junction of the detour and the off-road lane. He started back up, making his way through several thickly grown oaks, and when he came out on the far side, he noticed the small clearing with indentations of tire tread in its soft surface.

He hesitated, staring down at the clearing, then descended to check the tracks. Faintly evident in the pallid, early-morning light, they angled out of the clearing toward the detour road and appeared to have all been made by the same car. Their sharp imprint, and the condition of the gouged earth and squashed ground-covering, indicated they were relatively fresh, no more than a day or two old. One of the police or Highway Patrol cruisers? That seemed the likely answer. They'd pulled in here to make a run of the area without climbing down the knoll as he had just done.

Flagg turned to start upward again and a faint patch of blue caught his eye from a buildup of acorns and eucalyptus leaves directly in front of him. If he hadn't been looking right at it, he would have never seen it.

He went to one knee and brushed the leaves away and a moment later he held a small luminous blue triangle in the palm of his hand. It was about the size of a milk-bottle cap, of soft felt with an adhesive backing that was collected with dirt and bits of foliage now; on its face, in white, were the letters LL.

Flagg knew what the triangle was: a gate badge, one which allowed visitors admittance to the restricted grounds of certain government-subsidized companies in the area. Companies like Lamont Laboratories —

LL.

He put the triangular badge in the pocket of his overcoat and climbed to the knoll again. He started his car, drove down to the detour road and followed it the rest of the way back to River Valley Road. A mile beyond that point, the enclosed grounds of Lamont Laboratories lay nestled between foothills, its green pastel buildings shining dully in the diffused sunlight.

He passed by the main entrance gate without slowing and drove to the outskirts of Martinez. He stopped at a restaurant there, went directly to the phone booth at the rear of the dining area and placed a collect call to Churlak at his office.

"I didn't get much," Churlak told him. "But it seems Trenotti was bartending at a joint called the New Old Lompoc House, in Sweetweed."

"Where?"

"Sweetweed, Oregon. On Route 62, near Medford."

"Medford, I know. Great fishing thereabouts."

"Well, it sounds to me like this Lompoc House caters to fishermen, tourists and truckers. A highway watering-hole."

"Anything else?"

"It's owned by Trenotti's ex-brother-in-law, a retired middle-weight named Morley Ogden. Boxed under the title of Monster Morley."

"Never heard of him."

"Not many have. Morley had a glass jaw down to his ankles. Anyway, Trenotti's sister left Ogden years ago, and God only knows where she is now. Not even sure of her name, though Gupper Wells thought it was Idalina. As far as we can tell, she's never contacted Trenotti or Ogden since the split. You want us to try and trace her?"

"Not yet. What've you got on Ogden?"

"Squeaky clean."

"Yeah, he would be," Flagg said. He thought for a moment. "Offhand, I'd guess Ogden was fronting for Trenotti. A felon can't get a liquor license in Oregon, so it could be that Trenotti was a secret partner, using the tavern as an investment for his—profits."

"Then maybe Ogden tried pulling a fast one on him, eh?"

"It's possible—anything's possible, especially between relatives—but the odds on it are lousy. I can't see it's worth a trip up there to check out, not until everything down here is covered."

"Well, figure on going. I might as well break it to you now: I'm sending you up that way almost as far, to Grants Pass."

"How come?"

"Another of our DynaFreight trucks was jumped last night."

"How's that tie to Trenotti?"

"Forget Trenotti for a minute and listen: The hijackers got a shipment of cookers, a whole load of brand-new mash cookers and all the crap that goes with them. And that's bad, damned bad. Without the cookers, we can't expand our production in the Northwest on schedule; we'll lose customers, give that bastard independent outfit that's been undercutting us up there a chance to weasel more of a hold in our territory."

"You think maybe they're involved in the hijacking?

The outlaw moonshiners, I mean?"

"Maybe," Churlak said. "That's one of the reasons I want you on the job. You've been in on the bootlegging thing since it started, off and on."

Flagg sighed. The "bootlegging thing" had been frustrating the Organization for close to a year. An outlaw distiller was undercutting the Organization with his own raw copy of Old Pilgrim, the most commonly used house bourbon in the Northwest and Northern California. So far, Flagg and other Organization troubleshooters had been able to track the production to somewhere in southwestern Oregon; but after months of abortive footwork, backtrailing large purchases of grain and sugar and grid-checking the wild, mountainous terrain in low-flying planes, it had failed to locate any sign of activity in isolated places, any telltale columns of smoke or pollution in streams that could help it pinpoint the cooker.

Obviously, the distiller was taking great pains to conceal his still. And just as obviously, he was distributing his bootleg out of the area, perhaps out of California and Oregon altogether, shrewdly making it that much harder to trace. Otherwise, the Organization's men would have been able to find a local outlet that they could backtrack from.

"Where did the cookers get hijacked?" Flagg asked.

"Up near the Oregon border. Same general area the other hijacking took place."

The other hijacking had been of a rig full of furniture, a regular haul, and the Organization had figured it for a gang of outsiders. Now Churlak wasn't so sure. And maybe he had good cause to be dubious. It could be a random hijacking, but it could also be the outlaw distiller who was behind it, to set himself up with fresh equipment at Organization expense. If that was the case—and even if it wasn't the case—there was also the possibility of it being an inside job.

"The DynaFreight people are following up on the outside angle," Churlak went on, "but I want you to check the inside angle. So I'm arranging for you to slip in undercover, driving one of their rigs."

"Right away?"

"Finish the Trenotti thing first. Just be quick about it."

"Right. I've got something on it now."

"What have you got?"

Flagg told Churlak about the gate badge he had found, how he thought he might take advantage of it. He told him what he would need and Churlak said all right, he could have the stuff ready for him by eleven at the latest, and named a drop in Oakland.

Flagg said, "This might be a dead end, too. I'm still grabbing at straws."

"Keep after it," Churlak told him. "I'll be here the rest of the day, until about six, in case something pops."

"Fine," Flagg said. He hung up and went out into the dining area and ordered breakfast.

While he was waiting for it, he thought about the way Churlak handled things. Swiftly, decisively, without fanfare and without a lot of unnecessary violence and emotion, the way the Organization itself had become over the years.

Flagg liked the free hand Churlak gave him; he didn't care to work under pressure. True, Churlak had sounded a little more pushy about DynaFreight than he normally did when giving assignments, but Flagg understood why and didn't envy Churlak the pressure he must be feeling. The Organization owned controlling interest in DynaFreight and for the most part kept it as a holding company for tax purposes; but it had a massive investment in the nation-wide trucking concern and frequently used it to ship goods other than innocuous heavy freight. So by stealing the cookers, the hijackers had not only disrupted a profitable bootleg operation, but had also put in jeopardy the Organization's entire transportation network.

Yet as important as the DynaFreight problem was, Churlak hadn't arbitrarily pulled Flagg off the Trenotti deal before he could follow it through. Trenotti was important too, if not as much. For a ten-percent cut, the Organization had bankrolled his heist and promised him protection. Nobody could have foreseen such a foul-up as had happened, but still, as a result the one hundred and eleven thousand now belonged to the Organization—and so did Trenotti's killer, one way or another. It didn't look good for an Organization-backed man to be wiped out, his murderer to go scot-free. Word gets around about things like that, and enough words can spoil a reputation.

Which was why Churlak had called in Flagg. Flagg was the Organization's chief west-coast troubleshooter; he had their full support, usually unquestioned, and carte blanche for whatever information, materiel and even manpower he might need whenever he needed it. And to a man like Flagg, that made all the difference.

He finished his breakfast, had a second cup of coffee and drove to Oakland. The item he had requested from Churlak was waiting at the drop when he checked it at ten-forty.

THREE

Flagg eased to a halt at the main entrance to Lamont Laboratories a little past noon. He rolled down the window and smiled as the uniformed guard left his cubicle and approached the car.

"Afternoon," Flagg said pleasantly.

The guard nodded. "Afternoon." He had asthma and breathed heavily with his mouth open. "Can I help you?"

"I'm here to see Bernstein, in Security," Flagg said.

The guard nodded again and gave him a shiny blue triangle similar to the one Flagg had found earlier. "Main building's to your left, last one in the row. Be sure to sign the register when you get inside, and wear the badge on your lapel at all times."

"Right."

Flagg attached the badge to his jacket and drove to the building, where he parked in the visitors' lot. Inside the building's tile-and-glass-enclosed lobby, a tall girl with raven hair sat behind a receptionist's desk. There was a black leather register on the counter in front of her. She watched as Flagg signed it.

"Oh yes, Captain Gillrath," she said, turning the

register so that she could read it. "Mr Bernstein is expecting you. I'll tell him you're here."

"Thank you," Flagg said.

She picked up the phone on her desk, dialed a number and spoke briefly into the receiver. Three minutes later Bernstein came out. He was thin and angular and what little hair he had left was distributed in a vain attempt to conceal his spreading baldness. He shook Flagg's hand gravely. When Flagg flipped open the identification wallet Churlak had supplied him with, Bernstein glanced at it in a cursory way.

Flagg wondered if it was worth all the trouble the Organization had to go through to make up a false ID—especially one that said he was a state police captain—when people seldom even looked at it. But then he decided that the first time he went in without it, some guy like Bernstein would ask to inspect his credentials.

He followed Bernstein through a cell block of partitioned offices to a slightly larger one at the far end. Bernstein sat behind his functional grey-metal desk, indicating a modernistic chair to one side for Flagg. He leaned forward on his elbows and made a church steeple of his hands.

"I'm not sure what more I can tell you aside from our conversation on the phone, Captain," he said when Flagg had seated himself. "Our regular employees wear either orange or yellow squares, of a more permanent kind you pin on; and delivery trucks get green circles from the South Gate. But salesmen, government inspectors, everybody else visiting Lamont Labs gets a blue triangle, and we must hand out over a hundred a week." He made an apologetic gesture toward Flagg's lapel. "You were given one yourself."

"Then the only record of incoming visitors is that register I signed at the receptionist's desk?"

"I'm afraid so. It's like I said when you called, we aren't overly concerned with security. There's no top-secret cloak-and-dagger work here, and so we've no need for clearances and the like. We use the different colors and shapes as personnel control, that's all. Generally, it's only when somebody wanders into a section with the wrong color that they come to anybody's attention."

"Can people wander in and out of the building as easily?"

"Not really. The only entrance is through the lobby, the way you came in, and the person you want has to be called to come and escort you beyond there. That's been a long-standing Lamont policy."

"I see," Flagg said. He rubbed his left ear. "Could I look at yesterday's register sheets, if it wouldn't be too much trouble?"

"Of course," Bernstein said. He got to his feet and walked to the door. "I think my secretary has them. I'll be right back."

Flagg sat there and stared at a faded print of three mallards in a pond which hung in back of Bernstein's desk. Then he got out his pipe and packed it and lit it, and thought about the blue badge and wondered again why the Herald driver's pistol had been fired.

Bernstein returned carrying a manila folder. "Understand, these sheets aren't very reliable," he said, handing the folder to Flagg. "Visitors just sign in automatically, and they could put down any name they wish, or none at all, if Miss Osgood, our receptionist, happens to be away from her desk. They're never checked that closely."

"Uh-huh. Just another long-standing Lamont policy?"

"Well, yes. Maybe two or three times a year some salesman will call us for verification that he was here when he said he was, or the salesman's boss will call for the same reason."

Flagg opened the folder and looked at the top half-dozen sheets inside. Like the one he had signed earlier, each had been mimeographed with columns for *Name*, *In Time* and *Out Time*, *Person Visited* and *Company Represented*. On the top of each was the previous day's date.

He scanned the six sheets carefully, asking questions when he came to an entry which was illegible or sparked his curiosity. Near the bottom of the third page, he came upon a childish backhand scrawl.

"This one," he said. "Grady, is it?"

Bernstein squinted at the page. "Looks like that's the name, yes. From Herald Armored Car Service, here to see Jack Culp in Accounting."

"Can you get Culp in here?"

"Right away," Bernstein said, picking up his phone.

Culp was shaking hands with Flagg less than five minutes later. He was a small thick-set man who seemed a little nervous. Flagg showed him the register sheet and asked him about this Grady from Herald.

"Yes, I know him," Culp answered. "First name is Richard, but we call him Rudy. That's because he has a red face; always looks like he's blushing, if you know what I mean."

"Why was he visiting you?"

"Oh, Rudy helped us handle the payroll and bookkeeping. We have our own staff—I'm head of that section—but Herald sends out young men from time to time to help train them for their accounting service, which is a subsidiary of their regular business."

"Grady didn't come in an armored car, then?"

"No, no," Culp said. "He never carried any money or anything of real value, so he would arrive a little after the car in one of the company station wagons. You know the kind; they have the Herald shield on the door, but a sign beneath it saying that there isn't anything but records inside."

Flagg nodded, looking at the *Time* columns on the register sheet. "Grady was here from ten-forty to half-past three yesterday, right?"

"Well, I don't know about that. I didn't see him until I got back from lunch, which was sometime around one."

"Can anyone else verify that he was here from ten-forty until you saw him at one?"

"I couldn't say. He was in the lobby waiting when I—"

"He was, was he?" Flagg turned swiftly to Bernstein. "Would you get me the receptionist on your phone?"

Bernstein complied and Flagg said to the girl: "Were you on duty yesterday?"

"Yes."

"Do you recall a Richard Grady from Herald arriving?"

"Grady? Oh yes, Rudy."

"Who met him?"

"Why, it was Mr Culp, I suppose." There was a pause and then she said, "No, it seems to me that he signed in as he usually does, but when I mentioned that the armored car hadn't arrived yet, he frowned and said something about forgetting some books. He went out and that was the last I saw of him until just before Mr Culp returned from lunch at one—and took him in."

"Thank you," Flagg said. He hung up and said to Bernstein, "I'd like a duplicate copy made of this sheet . . ."

Fifteen minutes later, Flagg was on his way to Oakland again.

He arrived there just at two, threaded his way through the early-afternoon traffic and parked in front of the telephone company on 9th Street. In the lobby, he went through every directory within a radius of fifty miles. He found seven Gradys, Richard or R., in the nine Bay Area counties.

He went down the street to a luncheonette and changed two one-dollar bills into dimes. Then he came back to the telephone company and began calling.

By two forty-five he had narrowed the list down to two: Richard Grady, in El Cerrito; and R. D. Grady, in San Francisco. The other five had checked out negative; the phone had been answered at each of them, by four women and an old man with a cracked voice, and none of them knew a Richard Grady who worked for the Herald Armored Car Service. There had been no answer at the two he had left.

Since El Cerrito was on this side of the Bay, Flagg decided to check that one first. He got onto the freeway and drove north, exciting at the first El Cerrito off-ramp. He stopped for a map at the first service station he saw, found the street he wanted on it, and ten minutes later he was in the foyer of a new apartment building.

He rang the bell marked *Manager;* an answering buzz let him into the building. He showed the thin, hatchet-faced woman who descended the stairs the ID Churlak had gotten for him, and said he was looking for a Richard Grady who worked for Herald Armored Car Service on a police matter. She told him that the Richard Grady who lived there was with the Merchant Marine and had been at sea for the past two months. Flagg thanked her and got his car and headed for the Bay Bridge.

If he drew a blank at this last one, in San Francisco, it had to be that the Grady he wanted either didn't have a phone or, if he did, had an unlisted number. Or there was the possibility that he lived outside the fifty-mile radius Flagg had checked. But Flagg didn't think that was likely, considering the location of Herald.

The San Francisco address was a two-storied Victorian house on Fulton, across from Golden Gate Park. The house had been split so that each of its stories was a privately contained flat, with twin front doors facing the Park and the continual flow of traffic on Fulton. That wasn't good, as far as Flagg was concerned. He decided to see if any rear entrance was set up any better.

31

He parked his car on Eighteenth Avenue and opened the trunk. He took out a clipboard, a sheaf of gas-meter tabulators and an identification card that said he was George Axley, a meter-reader with Pacific Gas & Electric. He had found occasion to use these props often enough in the past to carry them regularly.

He walked up to the house, climbed the stairs to its broad front porch. There were twin mailboxes and doorbuzzers mounted on the post between the two doors, the one for the ground floor marked *Grady* and the other marked *Cheshire*.

Flagg pressed the buzzer for Grady and waited. There was no answer. He moved down off the porch, walked a block to the nearest payphone, which was in a corner drug-store. He looked up Cheshire in the directory, found a listing and dialed the number.

A woman's sleepy voice answered on the fifth ring. Flagg told her he was a lawyer named Simmons and that he was trying to locate a Richard Grady who worked for Herald Armored Car Service, to talk to him about a bequest from a maiden aunt in Schenectady. Was that the Richard Grady who lived downstairs from her?

The woman said yes, it was. Flagg thanked her and hung up, before she could think to ask how he'd gotten her number.

He returned to the block and began reading meters for the first four buildings. He had to go into the rear yards each time to do so and at the second one a fat woman who smelled of Chianti came out and he had to show her the PG&E identification.

When he stepped into the back yard of Grady's

place, he glanced up at the windows of the second floor flat to make sure the Cheshire lady wasn't looking out. They were curtained and empty. High wooden fences screened the yard from neighbors on both sides and from the houses whose small yards were directly to the rear.

He had another look around and satisfied himself that he was unobserved. There was still a risk in what he was going to do, but it had to be taken; Churlak paid him to take risks and he would be there with a brace of attorneys if Flagg took a fall for anything. He went up to the rear door, taking a strip of celluloid from his pocket.

It took him an hour to search Grady's flat. He found nothing except evidence that Grady was a bachelor with a well-stocked bar, an expensive stereo outfit, an address-book listing several dozen women, and a wad of dirty underwear under his bed. And that he *was* an employee of Herald Armored Car Service, as the check stubs Flagg found in a desk drawer helped to confirm. But there was no sign of the money. Wherever Grady had it—if he had it—it wasn't here.

Flagg left the way he had come in, quietly and unobtrusively. Nobody stopped him, nobody looked at him twice. He walked back to his car, put his clipboard, tabs and phony ID away in the trunk and took out an old army blanket and a paperback novel. He went across the street into the Park and spread the blanket out on the grass beneath an oak tree, directly opposite Grady's flat.

It was more than a bit nippy by then, but nearby were a few collegiate types tossing a frisbee, and two old men sitting cross-legged with a chessboard between them. Flagg settled on his blanket, facing Grady's flat, and opened the paperback to where he'd dog-eared the last page he'd read.

The book was a western. Flagg disliked westerns as a rule, which was why he picked them for stake-outs. They kept him from becoming bored, yet didn't interest him enough to absorb his attention. But this one, *Ghost Raiders of Superstition Cemetery,* was one of the worst pieces of crap he'd ever tried to wade through, so mostly he waited by watching the frisbee players and listening to the traffic pass on Fulton.

It was a long wait.

FOUR

Grady got home at six-thirty, when it was completely dark.

Flagg's attention was first drawn to the car, a two-year-old GTO painted a fluorescent racing orange. Traffic had thinned considerably by then and the driver geared down with a loud report from his dual exhausts, as he coasted by in the far right lane, looking for a parking space.

It was Grady, all right; Flagg could see him clearly enough in the light from the streetlamps: he was just as Culp had described him, carroty-red face and all. He went up to Seventeenth and turned. Flagg sat where he was and listened to the GTO being parked on the street.

A few moments later, Grady came walking around the corner. He moved splay-footed, looking neither right nor left. He went up on the porch, checked his mail and entered his flat. Lights flicked on, but the shades were drawn, then, so Flagg couldn't see any more of him.

Flagg got up and went back to his car. He put the blanket and the paperback away in the trunk, walked around to Seventeenth to where the GTO was parked. There were no other parking places in the block and there weren't any in the next block either. So instead of moving his car around, he sat down on the stoop of another Victorian nearby, took out his pipe and tobacco and waited some more.

A half hour passed. Then a woman came down the street and got into an old black sedan at the curb. Flagg hurried back to his car, circled the block and parked in the vacated parking spot. The GTO was five cars ahead of him now, on the opposite side of the street. He relit his pipe and settled down to wait again. He could afford to wait; he didn't think Grady could.

His wait lasted a little better than two hours. He switched on the car radio at eight to listen to the news, and Karensky was still at large. But the police would pick him up before long, Flagg knew; Karensky didn't have a prayer of escaping all the way to Mexico.

When Flagg saw Grady turn the corner into Seventeenth and walk to the GTO, he sat up straight on the seat. Grady had changed from his work clothes into polyester plaid slacks and a vinyl suede jacket; and his hair was fluffed out as though he'd just finished shampooing and blow-drying it. He seemed to be preoccupied; his movements were quick and jerky. He got into the GTO. Flagg gave him a block lead, then pulled out after him.

The tag was easy. Grady drove a little faster than the flow of traffic, which itself was going a little faster than the posted speed limits. He drove just the way Flagg pictured him to be: impatient, impulsive, a bit conceited and basically blind to what was going on around him.

The direction he was heading was south. Did he have the money cached somewhere down on the Peninsula, instead of in San Francisco or over in the East Bay? Or was he on his way to some other kind of rendezvous? It all depended on where and how well he had cached the money, and how long he would be able to keep his hands off it. If he didn't go to the money on his own initiative tonight, or at the latest tomorrow, Flagg would have to find a way to rattle him into doing it.

They continued down Bayshore, passed the International Airport and turned off on the Broadway exit in Burlingame. They angled southwest, through the placid, middle-class bedroom community, until they reached Cabrillo Avenue, where Grady turned left and almost immediately pulled in at the curb in front of the Seville Arms Apartments.

Flagg, a good two blocks behind, had no trouble easing to a stop just before the intersection. From where he parked, on the right side of Broadway, he had a clear view of the three-storey brick apartment house. He watched as Grady pushed the button under the mailbox for one of the units, waited for an answering buzz and then entered.

Flagg debated whether or not to cross over and find out whose name was on the mailbox. He decided not— at least, not until he was sure he wouldn't be caught doing it. And he was glad he hadn't; two minutes later. Grady came back out of the apartment house with a young woman in tow.

She was in her mid-twenties, Flagg judged, but it was hard to tell in the poor light. She was short, with heavy hips and breasts too large for her height. She was rouge-cheeked and mascara-eyed and her hair was straight and shiny and the color of dark wheat. She was talkative, too, showing a set of perfect teeth; and animated, gesturing constantly, tugging and stretching a size-too-small dress the pattern and colours of Christmas wrap.

The woman got into the GTO without any help from Grady. He started the engine, gunned it, showed off for her by peeling rubber. At the end of the block, he turned left onto Carmelita as Flagg pulled out after him. By the time Flagg reached Carmelita, Grady was three blocks down, turning right onto El Camino Real. Flagg increased his speed, jockeyed into a position a few cars behind the GTO, where he could keep tabs without being too noticeable.

El Camino Real was a four-, sometimes five-lane strip running south of San Francisco to San Jose. Like every other strip in every other urban area, it was a motorized carnival—the steady drum of exhausts and revved engines, the throbbing pulse of acid rock from eight-track auto stereos, the rhythmic red and yellow and green winking of traffic signals. And all around them, the fast-food chains and cocktail lounges and go-go discos like side-show vendors hawking unkept promises—buy, don't browse; buy, don't touch.

Flagg hated the claptrap of El Camino; he thought that maybe he should have stayed back by the Seville Arms until Grady returned with the woman. The way it looked, he was out on a goddamn date. But Flagg couldn't take the chance, no matter what the odds. There was always the chance that the woman was also

Grady's accomplice, and that he would take her with him when he went after the money.

The GTO crossed the line into the next community, San Mateo, and pulled into the parking lot of a place called Adnoid's. The lot was pretty full, but Grady found a spot after cruising around back of the low, naturalwood-and-neon building. Flagg passed him and parked a little farther on. He watched them enter through the rear doorway; he didn't have to follow to know what it would be like inside, or that he wouldn't like it. He could hear deafening rock-and-rut music coming through the walls, and joints with cutesy names such as this one always irritated him; he preferred an honest drink at an honest price in quiet surroundings.

Flagg followed the couple in anyway. They might be planning to meet somebody; besides, staying outside in his car risked being seen and rousted by the local cops.

He paid a five-dollar cover charge and for the next three hours endured two weak whiskeys and uninterrupted noise. Adnoid's was a disco palace, with Altec-Lansing "Voice of the Theater" speaker systems mounted in each corner, a disc jockey who laughed like a hyena between numbers, and a pair of topless dancers suspended in gilded cages. Postage-stamp tables surrounded a mirrored dance floor, which was bombarded by multi-coloured strobe lights and projections of old Tom Mix silent Western movies. The floor was packed with women quivering, churning, jerking and panting in near-sexual frenzy; and with men who for the most part did what Flagg thought of as the Dogshit Shuffle—a sort of jerky series of steps, as though they were trying to scrape dog turds off the soles of their shoes.

Grady and his woman didn't meet anybody. They drank and danced, drank and danced, Grady scraping his shoes and the girl shimmying and twisting and pouting her lips as if trying to communicate passion. Close to midnight, Grady appeared to believe the message; during one of the few slow numbers, he kissed her on the neck until she eased him away. His jacket was off by now and she fingered the gold medallion he wore on a chain under his unbuttoned brown shirt. Grinning, he hurried her off the floor, paid their tab, grabbed his jacket and propelled her outside.

By the time Flagg got out and into his car, they were gone.

He drove fast to the parking lot exit. He had two choices—the two directions of El Camino Real—but without hesitating he turned north, back toward the Seville Arms. Grady could be taking the woman to his cache, but it didn't look that way; it looked like he was simply out on the town with his fox, and that what he was hot after right now was sex, not the money. Which meant his place or hers, and hers was closer.

Whatever he was after, Grady wanted it in a hurry. Flagg didn't see the GTO again until he reached Broadway and Cabrillo and spotted it parked alongside the Seville Arms. Grady and the girl were already entering the building, their arms tight around each other.

The space where Flagg had parked before was now taken by a Datsun pickup. He cruised down Cabrillo, eased to the curb a hundred feet from the end of the Seville Arms. Adjusting his rearview-mirror so he could watch its entrance behind him, he settled in for the wait.

In one respect, he was better positioned here than before. The woman apparently lived on this side of the building: lights flashed on in a second-floor rear apartment, and he was sure she was the one he saw rolling the blind down in the lighted window. He twisted on the seat for a better look at that window. Nothing happened for several minutes. Then what Flagg assumed to be Grady's shadow moved into dark outline against the shade; it appeared to draw the woman's silhouette closer, rise above it, then merge into one form. The form glided away from the shade and the lights winked off.

The apartment stayed dark for over an hour. Flagg whiled away the time slouched on the front seat, eyeing the rearview-mirror and listening to the crackpots phoning in to KGO talk-radio. He felt bored yet keyed up, irritated that Grady was more interested in the woman's sack than the damned money-sacks. Some guys had no sense of priorities . . .

When the light came on, it caught his attention and turned him on the seat. It was a light in a different room—the kitchen, Flagg thought. Again, there was nothing for him to see for two or three minutes. Then the woman appeared for an instant, disappeared, appeared again. She was naked, one arm cradling her heavy breasts; the other hand held a telephone receiver pressed to her ear. What she was doing was pacing while she talked, in quick agitated movements. The conversation didn't last long. In less than a minute she disappeared from the window for the last time and then the light went off again.

The apartment stayed dark for another hour. The only thing that broke the tedium was one of the other tenants leaving to collect a pizza. When Flagg first saw the man come out of the front entrance, he figured him to be some sort of worker on a graveyard shift—a blue-collar worker, probably, because he was big and muscular and dressed in Levi's and a leather jacket. The man went around to the tenants' parking lot, got into a beat-up '65 Buick Wildcat sedan and drove away. Flagg thought no more about him until he returned fifteen minutes later and parked his Buick. When he got out he was carrying one of those wide, white pizza boxes; he disappeared with it inside the Seville Arms. Again, Flagg lost interest. If the man wanted a snack while watching the late show on TV, that was his business, not Flagg's.

Shortly before two a.m., the light in the front room of the woman's apartment came on again. The shade stayed down and shadowless and the light stayed on. Ten minutes later, Grady came out through the front entrance, carrying his jacket in his left hand, tucking in his shirt-tail with his right. For reasons of her own, the woman hadn't wanted him to spend the night. But Flagg wasn't surprised; if his assessment of her was correct, that kind of woman was little better than a whore anyway.

Grady drove away a lot more quietly this time and Flagg didn't wait so long before falling in behind. It was obvious by now that Grady was oblivious to the possibility of a tail.

Where to, now? Flagg wondered. If Grady headed

straight home to San Francisco, it would mean a long, sleepless stakeout because of the risk of the kid's slipping away. Flagg could call Churlak for a back-up team to relieve him, but he didn't want to do it. Basically, he was a loner. He liked being answerable to only one man, and to ask of that man only the information and supplies necessary to carry out his assignment; he worked best that way and his reputation was built on it. Reputation and discretion—that was the bottom line, just as it was in every other profession.

There were two other alternatives. One was going in after Grady, bracing him, roughing him up if necessary to get the whereabouts of the money out of him. But Flagg didn't want to do that, either. It was too risky, for one thing; and for another, neither he nor the Organization liked to use violence except as a last resort. The third alternative was rattling Grady, scaring him enough to make him run for the money. An anonymous telephone call might do that, and there were other ways as well. The only problem with that approach was that it might take days, and Flagg didn't have that much time; the police could get onto Grady at any time. He had to get the money before the cops got Grady or he might not get it at all.

Grady drove straight up the Bayshore past Candlestick Park. It looked to Flag as though he were on his way home, all right—but only until they neared the approach for the Bay Bridge. Then Grady swung over that way, passed the last San Francisco exit and headed out across the bridge. Flagg began to feel a little less grim about his prospects. And better still when Grady turned toward Sacramento on Interstate 80, then exited at Martinez. It looked, now, as though he were heading straight for River Valley Road.

There was almost no traffic and Flagg dropped farther back. But Grady continued to drive the way a man does when he's unaware of being shagged. When he reached River Valley Road, he swung onto and went on through the small town of Pacheco. Not far beyond its limits, his stoplights reddened and he veered to the right. Flagg slowed when he reached the intersection, peering off into the darkness. It was a road not much better than the one being used as a detour, maybe ten miles to the north of that one and Lamont Laboratories.

Flagg doused his headlights and turned onto the road. It was relatively straight, bounded by farmland on either side, but then the low, rolling Briones Hills began. At that point, the road began to curve and Flagg slowed to a crawl. His car had an extremely quiet engine, but he didn't want to take any chances that Grady would hear him coming on the curves and bypass the money.

That's what Grady was after; Flagg could sense it now. The kid had stashed it somewhere over here, after killing Trenotti, and he'd waited until it was nice and late before going after it tonight. There just couldn't be any other reason for a drive over here at this hour.

Flagg had gone almost two miles when he heard the GTO's loud exhausts as Grady downshifted, gunned his engine, then shut it off. When he came around a bend, cutting his own engine, he saw a small lane — little more than a pair of wheel ruts—that angled sharply down the slope on his left into a clump of oaks and eucalyptus.

A Lover's Lane during the summer months, probably, Flagg thought; a place Grady would be familiar with. He drifted to a spot off on the shoulder and switched off the ignition. He opened the compartment under the dash where he kept his arsenal, took out the woven leather sap. Then he stepped out, closing the door soundlessly behind him.

There was the steady, rhythmic chirp of crickets, but nothing else to hear. Flagg made his way slowly down the slope, blending into the shadows of the trees. When he came up to the edge of the clearing, he saw the GTO ahead of him with its trunk lid standing open. He stopped, listening.

On the other side of the clearing, in line with the GTO, he could hear soft scraping noises—rock against rock. He edged through the trees, around the rim of the clearing, taking his time. A pale yellow elongation of light pinpointed Grady's exact location. It came from a flashlight propped on top of one of three new but inexpensive leatherette suitcases. The beam was trained on a pile of small boulders, like a grave marker, which Grady was hastily unstacking.

Flagg waited until Grady had rolled away the last of the boulders. Then he went up and hit Grady on the back of his neck with the sap. Grady crumpled with a short, gasping sigh.

Right beside Grady, in a shallow depression which the boulders had covered, lay canvas sacks with the Herald emblem and name imprinted on them. Flagg didn't waste time checking what was in them, but sprinted directly to his car, drove it down to the clearing, and backed it around the GTO until it was next to the sacks.

He put on thin leather gloves, broke open the sacks one at a time and transferred the packets of banded banknotes they held to Grady's three suitcases. When the suitcases were full, he latched them and loaded them into the trunk of his car. Then he folded the now-empty sacks and wedged them in by the spare tire.

Leaving the trunk lid open, he went over to where Grady lay sprawled unconscious and searched him. In the pocket of Grady's jacket was the Herald service revolver which Flagg was sure had fired the bullet they'd found in Trenotti's neck. In his wallet were five receipts for safe-deposit boxes at five different Bay Area banks; and in the little fob pocket of Grady's trousers was an antique Elgin National railroad watch, still keeping good time, its dust cover enscribed: "G.T. — Happy Hours Forever!—M.O."

Flagg took the pistol, receipts and pocket watch to the trunk and packed them in one of the sacks, along with the photocopy of the Lamont register page which Bernstein had given him. He shut the trunk lid and went over to the GTO. He lifted its hood and removed the distributor cap, threw it far into the brush. Then he got into his car and drove out of the clearing.

It all meshed together now, he thought as he started back down the narrow road. The blue triangle had been the key, because it had opened up the possibility of the killer's being connected with Lamont Laboratories. When Flagg had seen Grady's name on the register, and learned of his routine and his unusual absence on the day of the heist, the pieces had all fallen into place.

The way Flagg surmised it, Grady had been ten or fifteen minutes behind the armored car, as per schedule. The skid marks and broken fence railing on the detour hadn't meant anything to him until he's learned the armored car hadn't arrived at Lamont. Flagg doubted that Grady had suddenly realized a robbery was taking place; more likely, he'd assumed there was trouble of some sort, and was covering for the company by checking it out before calling in.

So Grady had doubled back, figured out where the car had gone by the skid marks and railing and had parked in that clearing off the hiker's lane. He had gone quietly up the hill, seen what was happening, and that Trenotti was the only heister; and for some reason known only to him—maybe he was in debt, maybe it was just the lure of easy money—he had taken advantage of the situation by killing Trenotti and completing the heist himself.

The bullet fired from the driver's revolver now made sense, of a sort. Grady couldn't have known about Karensky, or that the police would figure the inside accomplice for the murder. So he'd shot the gun in a stupid attempt to misdirect the police, maybe even frame the driver, in the event they failed to apply a paraffin test to the driver's hands. It was something an amateur would try in order to cover himself—and it was almost as stupid as stealing the pocket watch. If Grady had taken care to check inside the watch's back cover, he would have realized the watch would convict him. It had obviously been given to Trenotti by his ex-brother-in-law, Morley Ogden.

But greed can blind a man. And Grady had been as blind as they come. He'd stashed the money sacks far enough away so that a general search wouldn't uncover them, but close enough so that he wouldn't be away from Lamont Laboratories for too long a time. Then he'd lain low the rest of the day and night. Today, once he felt Karensky was taking all the heat, he'd rented the safe-deposit boxes; tomorrow, if his plan had worked out the way he expected, he'd have put the money in them, waited six months or a year, and then quit Herald and gone off somewhere to spend the loot. He might have gotten away with it, too, Flagg thought—if Trenotti hadn't come to the Organization in the beginning.

But it was finished now, or almost finished. Grady wouldn't be going anywhere, except maybe to prison. Once Flagg got to Oakland—

Headlights came on suddenly, not far ahead, and another car spun into the narrow roadway from a concealed turnoff. It came fast, fishtailing, then straightening. Startled, Flagg stiffened, took a tighter grip on the wheel. The other car was less than fifty yards away now, still coming fast. Flagg, partially blinded by the glare of its high-beam lights, swung far to the right to leave plenty of room for the oncoming car to get by.

But the driver veered sharply toward him, as if out of control. Flagg couldn't get off the road because it was flanked by trees and undergrowth; he came down hard on the accelerator, with the idea of sliding past before the other car skidded into him. But he lost traction when his right rear tyre spun in the shoulder's soft earth, and he felt the rear end break away. And the dark onrushing shape cut toward him again, at an even sharper angle. Its driver was either drunk or bent on a deliberate collision.

Cursing, Flagg twisted the wheel, trying to regain enough control to slew clear. For an instant, he thought he was going to avoid impact and in that instant he recognized the other car in the wash of light from his own headlamps.

It was the old Buick Wildcat sedan that belonged to the rough-looking pizza-eater from the Seville Arms Apartments.

Then the Buick's massive grille crunched into the left rear quarter panel of Flagg's car, shearing into the sheet metal and ripping off chrome strips, and rammed the back end with enough force to spin it off the road into a tangle of trees and brush.

FIVE

The impact was jarring and glass sprayed Flagg when the rear window buckled and shattered, but he wasn't hurt. When the car stopped moving he struggled across the glass shards to the passenger door; he had no intention of going out the driver's side, because he wanted cover available when he faced the pizza-eater.

He shoved against the door, forced it open; the .38 Special was already in his hand. But he wasn't fast enough or lucky enough. Half-falling, half-stumbling, out into the brush, he felt a branch claw at his hand and dislodge the .38; it skittered away to his left, lost in the darkness. He caught hold of the fender to steady himself and when he did that he saw the looming figure of the big man standing beside the Buick's right front bumper. In one hand, glinting in the headlight glare, was a Colt .45 automatic.

There was nothing Flagg could do. He couldn't go backwards: the car was wedged against the trees from the rear tire to the rear bumper. And he didn't have enough time to go scrambling after the .38. He stayed where he was, with his hands up in plain sight.

"Christ, this ain't Dicky-boy," the big man said. But

he wasn't talking to Flagg; he was talking to somebody else inside the Buick.

"I told you, Earl," a woman's voice answered. "But you just wouldn't listen, would you?"

"Dark out here; I couldn't tell it wasn't the GTO. Who'd figure another car on a deserted road like this?"

Flagg had things worked out, now. They didn't have any idea who he was; as far as they were concerned, he was just a motorist who had gotten in their way. And that was the part he decided to play.

He said, "What's the idea of pointing that gun at me?" in a half-angry, half-frightened voice. The terror was feigned; the rage was genuine. "First you wreck my car, then you show me a gun. What are you, a bandit or something?"

The big man, Earl, moved forward a few steps, so that he was bathed in the light from the Buick's headlamps. He looked even taller and more muscular than Flagg remembered him. Scar tissue was prominent over his right eye, and his left ear was thickened and had a bulbous lobe. An ex-fighter, Flagg thought. Not very bright, probably, but cautious and full of animal instinct.

"All right, mister," Earl said. "Come on out here. Nice and slow."

Flagg obeyed, keeping his hands up at shoulder level. "I'm only carrying a few dollars," he said. "My watch isn't worth much, but you can have that if you—"

"Shut up," Earl told him. Then, without turning his head, he called over his shoulder to the woman, "Slide over and back my car free."

There was movement inside the Buick and the

woman's face appeared beyond the open driver's window. It was the overblown bimbo Grady had been with earlier, but Flagg wasn't surprised; he had figured that as soon as he heard her voice.

The woman said, "What about him?"

"You let me worry about him. Hurry it up, Verna, we're wasting time. Dicky-boy could come along any minute; we got to get set up again."

Flagg stood tensed, watching Earl's face, as the woman gnashed the Buick into reverse and began easing it free of Flagg's car. He didn't think the big man would try to kill him, not unless he was provoked or panicked. More likely, Earl would try to put him out of commission for a while. Long enough for Dicky-boy Grady to show up and get himself hijacked, just like he'd hijacked Trenotti. Only Grady wasn't going to show for some time and when he didn't Earl and Verna would start wondering about the only other car along this deserted road and if the motorist they'd hit was really so innocent. And if they wondered enough, they were liable to search his car and blunder right into the money they'd come here after. All of which meant Flagg couldn't afford to be put out of commission, not if he could help it.

The Buick pulled free with a series of loud scraping noises. The woman backed it up a few feet and stopped again: the high-beam lights were aimed straight at Flagg now, making him squint.

"Listen," he said to Earl, "I don't want any trouble. I'll give you whatever you want. I even got a bottle of whiskey in the glove compartment. Here, I'll show you . . ."

He half-turned, moving toward the driver's door of his car. Earl didn't say anything, but he came forward a few steps. He wanted Flagg turned around, would have ordered it in another few seconds, and Flagg wanted him up close; now it all depended on which of them was quicker. Flagg bent to the door, still half-turned, and made a pretense of trying to tug it open. Earl came gliding up behind him. Out of the corner of his eye Flagg saw the big man's arm raise, the .45 automatic turn sideways in his hand and come arcing downward like a bludgeon.

Flagg wheeled, ducking, snapping a stiffened left arm out and back on a horizontal plane. The automatic missed his head and grazed his left shoulder; his arm cracked against Earl's ribs with enough force to spin him and jerk his head back. Flagg hit him in the throat with a short forearm jab. Earl staggered, gagging and sucking for air, and the .45 popped free of his left hand and skittered under the Buick.

The woman had the car door open and was on her way out, shrieking and cursing. Flagg hit Earl twice in the face, left hand under the cheekbone, right hand on the point of the jaw; the big man reeled backwards, jarred into Verna before she could get out of the way, and they both went down in a tangle of arms and legs. The woman clawed herself free, up onto her hands and knees; Earl didn't move at all.

"You son of a bitch!" she screamed at Flagg. On all fours she scrambled back to the Buick and frantically began to sweep her arms back and forth underneath, trying to find the .45. "I'll get you, I'll fix you myself!"

Flagg went over to her. She was trying to crawl under

the Buick now; sobbing, ugly noises came from her throat. The hem of her dress had pulled up around her waist, exposing the plump cheeks of her ass. Flagg leaned down and caught hold of the bunched dress and yanked her out from under the car. She came up spitting like a cat, her fingers hooked into claws. Flagg hit her the way he'd hit Earl, on the point of the jaw and without pulling the punch any. He didn't try to catch her, either, when she fell. Hitting women was distasteful to him,—but this one was an exception. This one had been a pleasure.

He went around to the passenger side of his car, got the flashlight from the glove compartment and switched it on. It took him less than two minutes to find his .38. He holstered the weapon, then got into the car on the passenger side, wrenched the door shut and eased over under the wheel. The engine was still idling smoothly. He dropped the transmission lever into low, managed to rock the car free of the trees and shoulder. The resonator on the right side had broken, so the exhaust sounded louder than normal, but the crumpled fenders seemed to have taken the brunt of the collision, leaving the axles, differential and tires undamaged.

Flagg was relieved. If the car had been undrivable, he'd have been forced to take the Buick. And that would have meant dealing with Earl and Verna and he wasn't sure how he'd have handled things in that case. Tied them up, maybe, gagged them and put them into one of the cars, then somehow rigged a tow-line and hauled his car with the Buick to the nearest pay phone to call Churlak for assistance. His car would have ended up in an auto wrecker's crusher, and Earl and

Verna would have woken up in their Buick, parked out in the boondocks somewhere.

This way, with his car still operational, there was a lot less problem. He could just leave the two of them here. When they came to their senses they would get out of here on their own; they didn't know who Flagg was and they'd be worried that he might have gone to the police. Not that it mattered much, but they wouldn't be thinking any more tonight about Grady or the money.

Grady—dumb, dumb Grady, Flagg thought as he manoeuvred around the Buick and the unconscious figures of Earl and Verna, headed the car toward River Valley Road. Verna must have been two-timing him all along, and when he'd let it slip to her about his sudden wealth, she had notified Earl right away. That had probably been last night sometime. Then Verna had beguiled Grady into another date for tonight, taken him to bed and got him to reveal the approximate location of the money and the fact that he was going after it when he left her place. When Flagg had seen her talking on the phone in her kitchen, she'd been calling Earl to tip him off; that was why Earl had been up so late—he'd been waiting for the call. And once Grady was gone, she'd met Earl and the two of them had driven out here to waylay Grady, maybe even kill him—whatever it took to ensure that there wouldn't be any future problems with him.

Only their scheme, like Grady's, had blown up in their faces. That was because they were all amateurs trying to play in a professional league. Most amateurs were stupid, but this bunch was as stupid as they came.

They'd blundered in every way possible, including Earl and Verna calling each other by their right names in front of a witness.

They deserved each other and whatever happened to them. Earl was a dimwit; he'd wind up dead in an alley someday, or locked up in San Quentin, if he kept trying to pull strongarm stuff. Verna was a bitch, the worst kind. Flagg remembered the look on her face when Earl had been holding him at bay with the .45. If she had gotten her hands on the money, Earl wouldn't have lasted long in her plans, just as Grady hadn't lasted long. As it was, she would go on to screw up the lives of a lot of other men; and she'd wind up with one of them breaking her neck someday, or else as a fat old hooker hustling in cheap saloons.

As for Grady, the police would get him—Flagg would see to that—and he'd spend a decade or two behind bars. The idea pleased Flagg because he was convinced Grady had murdered Trenotti in cold blood. Trenotti was too old a hand to have bucked a young, excitable kid with a pistol, and he'd have kept very still and let Grady take whatever he wanted, figuring that later he would turn the matter over to the Organization to handle; that was what he'd been paying a protection percentage for. Greed and stupidity had killed him, and greed and stupidity would finish off Grady, too.

When Flagg reached Oakland he drove to a large suburban shopping mall and stopped at an all-night convenience store. He waited while a drunk bought a bottle of burgundy wine, then paid for a container of coffee and a giant economy twin pack of potato chips. Back in his car at the rear of the empty lot, he emptied the chips into the grocery bag and then got out and transferred the Herald money-sacks from the trunk to the cellophane wrapper that had contained the chips. Then he opened the coffee and used it to keep himself awake while he drove into downtown Oakland.

He parked a block from the Greyhound Bus Depot and walked back to it. Inside, he put the cellophane-wrapped money-sacks into a twenty-four-hour coin locker, stuffed the grocery bag with the chips and the empty coffee-container into a nearby trash-can. None of the sleepy transients awaiting late-night buses paid any attention to him.

In his car again, Flagg put on a pair of thin leather driving-gloves. Then he took an envelope from the glove compartment and addressed it to the Detective Bureau of the Oakland Police Department. On a slip of paper he wrote: *Key fits locker Oakland bus station. Concerning the Herald robbery. The man you're looking for is Richard Grady, a Herald employee.* He put the paper and key into the envelope, sealed and stamped and mailed it in a streetside mailbox.

As far as he was concerned, that put an end to his assignment. Churlak had instructed him to recover the missing money and take care of Trenotti's killer, and Flagg had done that in the new way of the Organization: legally and more or less nonviolently, with no clues to tie it back to the Organization.

When Grady regained consciousness out there on that lover's lane, he would have no place to go. He'd have to come out on foot and he'd probably make his way straight back to his apartment and hole up there; he was too stupid to figure out what had happened to him and the money, and too poor to pull up stakes and run for it. The cops would have him in custody within thirty-six hours. There would be questions about how the information Flagg had provided them was obtained, but Grady had never seen Flagg, so he wouldn't be able to tell them anything. And Verna and Earl sure as hell wouldn't come forward to volunteer information. Flagg had no police record and Bernstein's description of him, if the cops bothered to trace that far, would be useless.

Flagg drove back across the Bay Bridge into San Francisco. It was dawn by the time he reached his apartment on Russian Hill, and he was bone-tired. He mixed himself a bourbon-and-water, drank it while he stripped off his clothes. Then he called Churlak to report what had happened and to find out at which drop he was to leave the hundred and eleven thousand dollars.

He was in bed and asleep two minutes after he hung up the phone.

SIX

At five that afternoon, Flagg was on his way to Grants Pass to tackle the second assignment Churlak had given him—the DynaFreight hijackings.

He reviewed what he knew about them as he drove. Each of the two hijacked trucks had been found empty and abandoned in different isolated locations, which pointed to the use of a large van to transport the stolen goods to wherever they were being stored. The same two men had pulled off both jobs; the Organization had descriptions, but so far they hadn't been able to identify the men.

When the first hit had been made, Churlak and the other top men on the West Coast had chalked it up to a gang of freelancers who didn't know any better. But when the second hijacking happened in the same general vicinity, also of a load of masked bootlegging equipment, the Organization had begun to suspect there might be collusion. Swiping a legitimate haul of furniture was one thing; stealing a secret shipment of mash cookers and other distilling apparatus was just too damned convenient. Churlak mistrusted coincidence as much as Flagg did.

If it was an inside job, the suspects were few. John Villareal was the manager of DynaFreight out of Grants Pass, and an Organization man of long standing. So was Ben Lyons, his assistant. Those two knew that the Organization was freighting in the cookers along with crates of light industrial machinery—the only two who did know, outside a select hierarchy on the Coast. It figured to be one of them who was pulling a large-scale, and very foolish, double-cross. It could even be both of them together. Or neither of them, if the hijackings *were* coincidence after all, the work of an independent ring after regular merchandise for the black market.

In any case, Flagg was going in undercover to see what he could find out. Churlak had had to tell Villareal about him, or else Flagg couldn't have gotten the job or the run he'd wanted. But if it was an inside job and Villareal was behind it, Villareal still couldn't do anything. One move against Flagg, like having him conveniently killed during a hijack or in some sort of fake accident, and the Organization would know he was their man.

The car Churlak had supplied to replace his damaged vehicle handled well and Flagg arrived in Grants Pass late that evening, an hour ahead of schedule. He took a room at a motel, called Churlak again to check in. Grady had been arrested, Churlak told him, and had confessed almost immediately to killing Trenotti and heisting the money. The information had been supplied by Organization contacts in the police department.

Flagg said, "Did Grady tell them about getting

sapped last night?"

"He did. He thinks it was those two pals of his, the woman and the ex-pug; she was the only one he told where he'd hid the money."

"Do the cops believe him?"

"I doubt it. They're investigating, but they figure Grady's still got the money stashed somewhere."

"No problems, then?"

"No problems," Churlak said. "You handled it just right."

"Good."

"The cops picked up Karensky, too. It's all wrapped as far as we're concerned. Now let's see if you can wrap up the DynaFreight business the same way."

"I'll do what I can. Have you talked to Villareal?"

"He's expecting you first thing in the morning. Call me if you need anything."

"Will do."

Flagg broke the connection, took a shower and went to bed to catch up on his sleep. He was up at seven the next morning and in John Villareal's office at nine.

Villareal was a solid block of a man in his early sixties, with small, piercing blue eyes, a catfish mouth and cropped white hair. He wore work clothes, shirt open at the throat, the one concession to his position a wrinkled sports coat. He was sharp and shrewd, according to the reports Flagg had: a man who had started at the bottom and earned his way up through the ranks.

"Good to have you here, Flagg," he said. "Now maybe we'll get to the bottom of these damned hijackings."

Flagg said, "My name is supposed to be Eric Scofield. You'd better start calling me that in private so you don't slip in public."

"Yeah, you're right. Okay, Scofield—I've arranged for you to take the next run south to Frisco. When you get there you'll pick up a new load of cookers and equipment and bring it back up here."

"When do I leave?"

"This afternoon. The pickup is scheduled for tomorrow morning."

"What's the cover shipment?"

"Mixed stuff, most of it baby cribs."

"All right, good."

"You want me to take you around, introduce you to the other people here?"

"That'd be a good idea. Suppose we start with Ben Lyons."

"Sure. Ben's okay; I've known him a long time."

Flagg didn't say anything. He'd find out for himself if Lyons was okay; nobody's word was any good in a situation like this.

Lyons turned out to be fortyish, with an amused look in his eyes and a well-modulated tone to his voice that carried a hint of condescension. He dressed better than Villareal and he wore a diamond ring on one finger. It was obvious he liked money, but then a lot of people did; it didn't have to mean anything one way or another.

"DynaFreight's a good outfit to work for," he said. "I think you'll like it here, Scofield."

"I hope so, Mr Lyons," Flagg said.

The third DynaFreight employee he met was the

company dispatcher, Frank Northrup—a man in his early thirties, owner of a round face and a sprinkling of freckles across his nose and cheeks. Villareal told him afterward that Northrup had worked his way up to his current job in a very short time, called him a go-getter. A couple of the other drivers Flagg talked to later had a different term for him. "A brown-noser," one of them said. "I never met anybody kissed as much tail as Northrup does around here."

Flagg spent the rest of the morning familiarizing himself with the DynaFreight operation. The yard was good-sized, sprawling, with a half-dozen big rigs on the premises and another two dozen on the road, and two big storage warehouses. When Villareal and Lyons went out to lunch, Flagg slipped into Villareal's office and rummaged in his desk. There was nothing that pointed to Villareal as a potential traitor. Nor was there anything in Lyons's effects, Flagg discovered when he searched the assistant manager's office.

He spent a few minutes with the dispatcher, Northrup, to see if he could pry loose any information about Villareal and Lyons. Northrup was talkative enough, but he also seemed loyal; he didn't have any gossip to pass along. Still, Flagg didn't like him much—there was something a little secretive about the man. It was possible that Northrup, in his position as dispatcher, trusted employee and brown-noser, could have found out about the masked shipments of bootlegging equipment; that it was he, not Villareal or Lyons, who was the inside man on the hijackings. Flagg added him to his list of suspects, made a mental note to have Churlak check him out through Organization channels.

The rig he would be driving, a cab-over diesel semi, was loaded and ready for him by three o'clock. The load was another shipment of furniture—clean goods this time. He spoke to Villareal again before he left, to find out where to pick up the cookers in San Francisco. Then he climbed into the diesel's cab and headed it south.

When he reached San Francisco, he drove to the DynaFreight yard there and left the truck to be offloaded and then reloaded with the cookers and the other goods. He spent the night in his apartment, after checking in again with Churlak, and was back at the DynaFreight yard at six the following morning.

He spent a few minutes alone in the van, checking the shipment. The cookers, as had been the ones on the previous shipments, were in crates marked *Machine Tools*. Satisfied, he got into the cab and pulled the rig out of the yard, took it out onto the highway headed east for the swing up Interstate 5.

Okay, he thought as he drove. Now we find out if anything happens.

SEVEN

Something happened, all right.

He stopped for coffee at the Big Pine Cafe along Interstate 5, near the Oregon-California border, and when he came out a hijacker showed up hidden in the sleeper compartment of his rig.

He didn't notice anything wrong as he left the cafe and walked across the broad sweep of the parking lot. It was after ten, but the chill mountain air needled through his lined leather coat. The sky was clear again, after two days of monsoon-like rains that had inundated the Sierra Nevadas.

Flagg swung up into the driver's seat. The cab was still warm from his trip up from San Francisco; the diesel turned over immediately. He let the engine idle for a moment, shifted into the first of twelve forward gears, turned on his blinkers and slowly eased the growling Peterbilt rig out onto the highway.

He had driven no more than a quarter-mile when the cold muzzle of a gun jabbed suddenly against the nape of his neck. He stiffened, started to turn his head, and a sharp voice said, "Easy, just take it easy, buddy. Don't ask questions, don't try turning around. Just keep driving and do what you're told."

Flagg let his muscles relax, concentrating on the road ahead of him. Behind his seat was the small, curtained-off bunk used as a sleeper on long hauls. On shorter ones, it was used for storage, and Flagg had put a few things back there before leaving the DynaFreight yard in San Francisco. The cafe had been his only stop since then, so the man had to have slipped it while he'd been having his coffee.

Shifting gears carefully, Flagg watched the tach as the grade of the highway steepened. He thought of the stretch to come and knew that in a few miles there was an exit for a county road. Even at this hour of the morning, that road would probably be more or less deserted.

When they reached the exit, the hijacker prodded Flagg with the gun and said, "Turn off here." Flagg did as he was told. A third of a mile along the county road, a wide shoulder appeared, where trailers and trucks could pull over to allow strings of cars to pass.

The hijacker prodded him again. "Over on the shoulder. Park and idle."

Flagg downshifted, coasting the diesel along the shoulder and off the road. "Now what?" he asked, keeping both hands on the steering-wheel.

"I told you, don't ask questions."

They sat in silence for several minutes. Then a battered forest-green pickup truck pulled up in front of the cab-over and braked to a halt. Two men got out.

Flagg studied the pickup for any peculiarities which might help to trace it later. It was a five- or six-year-old Ford Ranger half-ton, already rusting out pretty badly, especially along the fenders and door sill. Its bed was empty, except for a set of ice-encrusted tire chains and some left-over snow clinging to the corners. Its rear license plate was mud-caked, no doubt on purpose. But other than a heavy-duty steel back bumper, and a fiberglass CB whip antenna mounted on its cab, there was nothing distinctive about the truck to identify from thousands of others.

The two men were in their thirties, Flagg judged as they approached the diesel. Each wore nondescript tan work pants and heavy plaid jackets. One had on a red hunting cap with the ear flaps pulled down. Both carried rifles in the crooks of their arms.

"Out," the man in the sleeper ordered.

Flagg opened the door and swung down. If the men weren't full-fledged pros, he thought, they were at least experienced enough to know what they were doing. The hijacker with the pistol had him under control; they didn't bother to level their rifles at him. The presence of the rifles was enough. If he tried to make a run of it, they could pick him off like a deer.

The man from the sleeper stepped down alongside him. He had bushy black eyebrows and a flattened nose; he wore a scarred brown leather bomber jacket, vintage World War II, and a dark blue wool cap, the kind seamen preferred. His pistol was a 9mm Browning automatic.

"No trouble," he said to the other two, in the same flat, bored voice he had used in the cab. Then he looked at Flagg almost disinterestedly and said, "Okay, driver, turn around."

Flagg turned around, putting his hands on the frigid

metal of the cab cowling. He could feel the vibrations of the idling diesel, and the throaty chug of its exhaust was loud in his ears—but not so loud that it drowned out the sound he was expecting. The sound came, a sharp rustling of the bomber jacket as the man behind him swept his gun arm up.

There was nothing Flagg could do. He stood tensed, his mind blank, waiting. And then there was a bright white flash just behind his eyes, as if a flashbulb had exploded, and that was the last he knew . . .

He regained consciousness slowly. He was cold and wet, and when he got his eyes open and focused, he saw that he'd been rolled off the pavement into a ditch. His clothing was soaked through and matted with grey slush. There was no sign of either the diesel or the Ford pickup.

He lifted a hand and explored the back of his head, wincing. There was a tender spot just over his right ear; he could feel the blood that had dried there. There were swirling shadows at the corners of his eyes and he wondered if he had a concussion.

Gingerly, he got to his feet. The sun, pale and diffused in the wintry sky, was nearing its zenith; it was almost noon. He'd been unconscious for a little over an hour.

On legs that were a little unsteady, he walked across to the highway. There was still very little traffic. He paused until his legs stopped shaking, then began hiking back toward the Big Pine Cafe.

It took him almost an hour and a half. When he reached the cafe, he went into the men's room and cleaned up as best he could, then sat down at the counter and ordered toast and a bowl of soup. The waitress gave him a curious stare but said nothing. By the time he finished the soup, some warmth had started filtering through him again. He ordered coffee, then went to the payphone that was in the hall beside the rest-rooms and called DynaFreight in Grants Pass.

When he got Frank Northrup on the line, Flagg said: "Listen, this is Eric Scofield. I've been hijacked a couple of miles south of Big Pine Cafe on Interstate 5. I'm calling from there now."

Northrup cursed softly and vehemently. "They take much?"

"The whole damn rig."

"And you? Are you all right?"

"They clouted me on the head," Flagg said. "You want me to call the cops?"

"I guess you'd better."

"Will anyone be coming down?"

"I'm sure Mr Villareal will be."

"Well, I'll be taking a unit in the motel here."

"You don't have to do that."

"Well, I am," Flagg said. "I think I might have a concussion, and if that's the case, I won't be in any shape to travel."

"We'll be in touch," Northrup said.

Flagg hung up, found another dime and placed a long-distance collect call to Churlak at his San Francisco office number. After Churlak accepted the charges, Flagg told him; "I just got hit."

"Where?"

"Up in the Sierras, near where the other two hijacks happened. There was a guy stowed in my truck's sleeper compartment when I came out of a place called the Big Pine Cafe. He had a couple of friends in an old green pickup tagging along behind, license plates muddied over. I got sapped with a gun butt and dumped in a ditch, and they got the truck."

"Damn! You okay?"

"Concussion, maybe. I'm going to see a doctor."

"Do that," Churlak said. "What were you carrying?"

"A mixed bag, mostly baby cribs."

"Baby cribs? Hell, that must mean they were after the shipment of cookers. Why would they make off with baby cribs?"

"It might be a random hit," Flagg said. "They might not have known what I was carrying, or bothered to check before they made off with the truck."

"Maybe. But I don't like the way this thing is shaping up."

"Neither do I."

"Same bunch of hijackers as before?"

"Looked that way, from the descriptions you gave me."

"Anything distinctive about them or the pickup?"

"I'm not sure," Flagg said. "I'm not thinking too clearly yet."

"Yeah, understandable. Does Villareal know?"

"I phoned DynaFreight, but the dispatcher was the only one I could get hold of. I told him and he'll tell Villareal." Flagg paused. "What do you know about the dispatcher, Northrup?"

"Why? You think he might be mixed up in the hijackings—the inside man?"

"I haven't turned up anything to make me think so, no. But he could have found out about the cookers and the other equipment; that makes him a possible."

"We checked him out when this all started," Churlak said. "Clean, as far as we could tell. I can try to dig deeper if you want."

"Might be a good idea."

"Okay, I'll take care of it. You going back to Grants Pass after you get a doctor to look you over?"

"I don't think so. There's a motel here, and I think I'll hole up in there for a day or so. The hijackers have got to be operating out of this area someplace; maybe I can dig up something useful."

"Fine. You need anything?"

"Wheels."

"What kind?"

"Can you manage a camper?"

"No problem. You want it fully outfitted?"

"Yes."

"It'll be on the way in a couple of hours."

"I'll keep you posted," Flagg said, and hung up.

He dialed the California State Highway Patrol, since the Big Pine was just south of the Oregon border and the hijacking had taken place in California. He reported what had happened and where he was. Then he went out and took a booth at the rear of the cafe, under a suspended unit heater. He was still cold and wet. He ordered more coffee and sat drinking it, waiting, letting his mind work on the hijackings again.

The one this morning of his truck made three in less than ten days—three straight shipments of bootlegging equipment. An outside group could still be responsible;

a gang unaware that they'd stumbled into Organization-controlled territory would keep right on hitting DynaFreight trucks until they thought it wasn't safe any longer—and each hijack had been pulled in a different fashion, in order to avoid traps or stakeouts. But if that was it, Flagg had a hard time figuring where things like furniture and baby cribs could be readily disposed of on the black-market.

No, Churlak had probably been right: they were after the cookers and the other apparatus. But then what would they do with them? Fencing equipment like that would be difficult and wouldn't bring them much cash return.

Well, there was one other possibility and it opened up a whole new can of worms. It could be that there was a connection between the hijackings and the outlaw still that was operating in southern Oregon ...

Flagg's thoughts were interrupted by the arrival of the Highway Patrol. They took him in a patrol cruiser to the nearest town, where he was treated and X-rayed at the local clinic. All the while, and on the drive back, the cops questioned him. Flagg was responsive and helpful, but there wasn't much he could tell them. He signed a report at a nearby substation and after that they returned him to the Big Pine Cafe and Motel.

He walked across to the motel end and rented a single. Inside his room, he stripped, showered and crawled into bed. His head still throbbed, but the doctor at the clinic hadn't found signs of a concussion; he had given him some pills for the pain. The pills put Flagg to sleep almost at once.

EIGHT

Flagg was awakened by a persistent knocking on his door.

He blinked rapidly several times, found that his headache was gone. He got out of bed and went to the door and let in John Villareal, who settled himself in the motel room's only chair. Flagg sat down on the edge of the bed.

"What happened?" Villareal asked.

Flagg went through it all again. Villareal sat listening stone-faced, without interrupting.

When Flagg had finished relating his account, Villareal said: "So those are the facts. Now, what's your opinion?"

"The hijackers knew exactly what they were doing."

"Nothing amateur about them, eh?"

"Well, they acted experienced enough. But I also got the feeling they were coasting."

"You mean that they didn't care?"

"Oh, they cared that the heist came off smoothly. They just didn't seem to care that I was hauling some pretty useless cargo."

"So you don't think they were after more cookers?"

"I don't think they were after anything in particular."

"Doesn't sound very professional, to blindly grab and run."

"Yeah, and it's puzzling."

"I guess, though, it shows nobody's fingering for them."

"Maybe."

"What else could it be?"

"Window-dressing."

"You can't be figuring this for an inside job!"

"I'm keeping an open mind."

"Believe me, there's no traitor at my end of things."

Flagg smiled faintly. "Let's hope not."

There was another knock on the door. Frowning, Villareal reached over and opened it. A well-dressed man Flagg had never seen before entered and asked, "Is an Eric Scofield here?"

Flagg nodded. "I'm Scofield."

The man tossed a set of car keys, which Flagg fielded with his right hand. "Camper's parked outside, down at the end in the last slot. It's fully equipped, including chains. Any message?"

"No. Thanks."

The man said, "Right," and backed out of the door, closing it behind him. Momentarily, there was the sound of a car pulling away on the motel's gravel driveway.

"Who was that?" Villareal asked.

"Delivery boy." Flagg rose from the bed to dress.

"You planning to stay on here?"

"For a while. I want to look around a bit."

"What the hell, I'll stay on, too. I'll call Grants Pass."

"Put me on sick leave while you're at it."

"Sure thing."

When Flagg had finished dressing, he and Villareal walked outside together. They agreed to meet for supper at the Big Pine Cafe, if nothing came up in the interim; then Villareal went across to the cafe to make his phone call and Flagg walked down the row of motel units to inspect the vehicle Churlak had provided him.

It was a newish Chevy three-quarter-ton pickup with an aluminium camper attached to its bed. As promised, it was fully stocked; there was even an AM-FM-cassette stereo installed in the cab.

The remainder of the day, Flagg spent touring in the camper. Mainly he stayed on Interstate 5, cruising south to Redding, then backtracking up into Oregon toward Medford. But he also travelled some of the secondary highways and branch routes, visiting various towns and hamlets like Castella, Montague, Talent and Phoenix. He stopped at every restaurant, service station and tavern along the way, asking if anyone had seen or knew of a trio of middle-aged men driving a battered green Ford pickup, or perhaps a large van.

Taverns offered him his best hope, he figured. Hijackers like these might not talk while eating or buying gas, but tongues had a way of loosening when oiled with liquor and a chance to brag. And in each tavern, Flagg ordered a shot of Old Pilgrim with a water chaser. He would sip the bourbon once, neat, for its flavour and texture. Then he would drink just the water, while he asked carefully veiled questions not only about the three men, but also about the tavern itself—if it had been there long; if business was gone; if taxes were killing; and especially if its wholesale suppliers were generous with discounts and deals. The Organization's troubleshooters had been over most of this territory already, looking for the outlaw distiller, but it was always a good idea to double-check just in case. And the opportunity was perfect for him to cover the two investigations at once.

He kept drawing blanks, but still continued to plug away. Just north of Medford, he turned off the Interstate and followed Highway 62 through rolling farmland and timbered foothills. Before long the highway began to parallel the Rogue River, which to Flagg's mind was one of the most frustrating, unpredictable rivers he'd ever fished. Soon as he'd find a choice spot for trout, the Rogue would live up to its name and shift it out from under him. He loved it.

Some thirty miles from Medford, Flagg arrived at Sweetweed. Sweetweed was hardly more than a wide stretch between the road and the river, consisting of two service stations, one with a garage; an antique-store crammed with junk; a closed-for-the-season cafe; a bait and tackle shop with a boat ramp; and the New Old Lompoc House.

Flagg pulled in beside the New Old Lompoc House, thinking how right Churlak had been when he'd called it a watering-hole. Set in a scraggly conifer grove and ringed by small, weathered tourist cabins, the House was a box-shaped, clapboard building with a slant-shingled roof and a falsely rustic façade. Flagg had seen dozens like it in the past few hours and he had begun to wonder if they were all produced from some master mold.

He opened the door and stepped inside. The barn-like interior was bathed in the eerie, reddish-tinged shine of the neon beer signs in the long front window. He glanced at the smattering of customers sitting at the wooden tables with their matching chairs, and at the glitter-decorated musicians' dais along the rear wall. Then he angled left and went to the long polished bar, where another four men sat hunched on their stools, nursing their drinks and ignoring one another. A radio behind the bar was blaring a twangy western tune.

Flagg sat down on a stool and waited for the bartender.

The bartender didn't come. He was down at the far end, leaning on the counter with his back to Flagg. He was talking to the cocktail waitress, who was standing with one foot hooked on the bar rail, her fingernails idly drumming her serving-tray.

Flagg couldn't tell much about the bartender, other than he had a fat behind and his shirt tail hung out. The hostess appeared to be a tall, pale woman in her mid to late twenties, her face a long oval noticeably lacking makeup around dark eyes and a small plump mouth; her taffy blond hair was arranged in two curved wings across her forehead and drawn back and fastened in a loose bun. She was wearing red knit tights and an outfit of even brighter red sateen, its hem cut almost at her crotch, its bodice cut low and straight across with just thin straps over her shoulders—a sort of 1928 Tart look, Flagg thought. Her figure, as revealed by the skimpy costume, was on the slim side, high-breasted and tight-butted, except for a potentially dangerous case of jodhpur thighs.

"Hey, Morley," one of the men at the bar called out, "how about a refill?"

The bartender moved slowly, almost reluctantly from the girl and served the man another glass of beer. The girl left the bar, went around to the tables to see if anyone wanted service; she walked with a careless, athletic grace, imparting a sensual sway to her body from the waist down. The bartender rang up the beer sale and turned to Flagg. "What'll it be?"

"Pilgrim, water back," Flagg said, and stared intently as though he'd seen the bartender before but couldn't quite place him.

The bartender poured and served. "Buck-fifty."

Flagg paid, still staring quizzically at him.

The bartender bristled. "What're you gawking at?"

"Aren't you Monster Morley, the middle-weight?"

"I was, yeah. What of it?"

"Nothing. Just thought I recognized you, is all."

"No kidding," Morley said. He gave Flagg a sour, suspicious glance, rang up the sale and waddled back down the bar to where the hostess was once more standing, tapping her tray.

Flagg rolled a bead of the bourbon around his tongue, savouring it, and thought that Morley Ogden's belligerence was to be expected. Aware of how Trenotti had died, Ogden would know he'd be on the shit list of every snoopy cop and federal agent with a bone to pick. Besides, he no longer resembled a boxer, even a bum one gone to seed. He was gross with flab, his face jowled and pink like rare roast beef, and he wore a toupee so patently fraudulent that it looked like he had on a hairy beret. Naturally he'd be on the defensive, and surly toward any stranger claiming to recognize him.

Too bad; the "Monster Morley" was Flagg's best gambit for opening a conversation. Now that that had failed, he could stay there all night and still learn nothing more from Ogden.

The bourbon, though, was something else again.

Literally.

Dusk was falling when Flagg left the New Old Lompoc House. He switched on his lights and returned to the motel, pausing briefly in Medford to fill the camper's twin fuel tanks and to telephone Churlak with a report and a request for a special set of fake ID. Churlak said that he couldn't promise on such short notice, but that he'd try to have the set in the camper's glove box by midnight.

Flagg arrived at the Big Pine to find Villareal waiting for him for dinner. Sitting with Villareal in a rear booth were two other men: One was Ben Lyons; the other was Frank Northrup.

Flagg sat down, keeping his face expressionless and his manner that of a rank-and-filer in the presence of brass. Northrup wanted to know how his head was and Flagg told him it wasn't as serious as he first thought.

"I didn't think so," Northrup said. "Saw you drive up just now, Eric. Nice camper you've got there."

"It's not mine," Flagg said. "My brother-in-law's. He lives over in Crescent City; letting me borrow it while I'm here."

"Some brother-in-law."

"It evens out," Flagg said. "My sister's a bitch."

They ordered dinner and a round of drinks. When the drinks came Northrup rose, excused himself and headed for the men's room.

As soon as he was out of hearing range, Lyons leaned across the table and said to Flagg: "John told me who you really are."

Flagg gave Villareal a hard look and the manager spread his hands apologetically. "I couldn't help it. Ben guessed the truth."

Lyons nodded. "Two hijackings, and suddenly we put on a new driver on the Interstate run. It was too much coincidence; I've been around too long not to figure out what was happening. I went to John, and he had to admit it. Don't blame him."

The hell I don't blame him, Flagg thought; Villareal didn't have to admit any damned thing at all. He asked him, "Who else knows?"

"Nobody," Villareal answered.

Flagg turned to Lyons. "What are you doing here? And why did you bring Northrup with you?"

"I came down because I'm as concerned as John about these heists," Lyons replied. He kept his voice soft, glancing in the direction of the rest rooms as he spoke. "And I brought Frank along so I could keep an eye on him. As John says, if there's a chance that the cargo's being spotted by someone on the inside, it'd more than likely be someone who wouldn't know about the cookers, but who would be able to tell the hijackers which legitimate hauls are valuable."

"Baby cribs are valuable?"

"Around L.A. and San Diego, they're dynamite."

"Don't forget you were also hauling some appliances and a few television sets," Villareal added. "I'd estimate the shipment could be dumped for eight to ten thousand, easy. Same for that first load of furniture, and there's been a steady black market for light industrial machinery, which is how the cooker load was manifested."

"There's more to it than that," Lyons continued. "If there is an insider working with the hijackers, he'd also have to know when the trucks'd be leaving, and what routes they'd be taking."

"So you've narrowed it down to the dispatcher?"

Villareal shrugged. "It adds up to him."

"Northrup's been with us the shortest time," Lyons said. His voice was still low but it had grown more intense. "And I've run across him some places around the yard where a dispatcher has no call to be. He's always had a ready excuse, but damn it, he's just too much of an eager-beaver—always asking questions, always hustling."

Flagg said, "What was his reaction when you asked him along?"

"Eager."

"That's hardly proof."

"For chrissake," Villareal said. "You think if we had him pegged solid, we'd all be sitting here gabbling about it?"

"So tell me more."

"I admit, we don't have anything concrete to go on," Lyons said. "Not yet, anyway—and that's still assuming we've got an insider fingering the loads. But that's why I want Northrup handy when we finally do get to the bottom of this—"

He broke off. Northrup was returning to the booth.

Villareal ordered a litre of burgundy to go with dinner and they settled down to that and to small talk with the food. They went their separate ways not long after the meal was over.

Flagg retired to his motel room. For a while he sat in one of the chairs, smoking his pipe, doing some mental work. The possibility that Frank Northrup was involved with the hijackers put a fresh slant on things, gave him a new angle that would bear investigation. Which he could take care of when he returned to Grants Pass, assuming nothing further developed around here. Yet there was something else, Flagg sensed; some small but significant fact which tickled the edge of his mind and then vanished before he could recognize what it was, what it meant.

He tried to jog his memory, dredged up nothing meaningful and finally pushed the whole problem aside. Undressing, he set the alarm of his travel clock, climbed into bed and willed himself to relax. It had been a long day, and his head was beginning to throb again, and there was still a long night ahead of him. Eventually he dozed off.

The alarm woke him at one a.m.

After a quick shower to revive himself, Flagg put his clothes back on. He went outside and walked noiselessly toward the camper.

The night was cloudy, with a crisp breeze coming off the mountains. The wide graveled expanse common to both cafe and motel was quiet; only a few people, mostly truckers, were in the cafe. The motel units

Villareal, Lyons and Northrup had rented were dark and silent and their cars were parked in the corresponding spaces.

The set of fake ID from Churlak was not in the glove box.

Flagg stayed in the camper, engine off, and waited. Churlak's messenger arrived at one forty-five, but that still left enough time, because the taverns in Oregon did not close until two.

Even leaving at two would get Flagg to Sweetweed before three-thirty. And three-thirty, he felt, was the earliest he could risk breaking into the New Old Lompoc House.

NINE

Flagg leaned against the camper's tire-iron until the hasp broke and the lock dropped to the pine-needled ground. He paused, listening, but the only sounds were the faint rippling of the Rogue River and the distant call of an owl in the surrounding woods.

After a long moment, he kicked the lock away, put the tire-iron against the wall and edged the door open. The light from the cloud-streaked moon illuminated nothing more than vague shadows in the black interior. Once he had stepped inside and pulled the door shut behind him, he took a small penlight from the pocket of his leather jacket and clicked it on.

He was in the rear storage room of the New Old Lompoc House.

Flagg moved deeper into the room, playing the flash. Along the near wall were cases of liquor and beer and mixers, and along the far wall were cartons of peanuts, potato chips, pretzels and other assorted snacks. He checked the liquor cases, opening a couple of them at random, and then went to a bank of shelves beside the entrance to the bar proper. Soap, disinfectant, cloth towels—but no sign of what he was searching for.

He opened the door and stepped into the bar. The neon beer signs were still on, casting their eerie if meager glow; and so was a bare, low wattage bulb dangling from a cord above the musicians' dais. That was all, though, so Flagg kept his penlight on. The planks squeaked beneath his shoes as he moved cautiously along the backbar.

When he reached the well where the bourbon was located, he picked up the bottle of Old Pilgrim from which he had been served that afternoon. He removed the pour spout and sniffed briefly at the neck. Then, for reaffirmation, he tilted the bottle to his lips and allowed a small amount of the liquor to wet his tongue.

It was the same: sour, yeasty, too young, not at all like the brand's high quality. Moonshine, and bad 'shine at that.

Flagg examined the bottle carefully, looking for the flaws he'd taken a crash-course to learn about. The glass had a few minor defects, but it was generally a good replica of the real Old Pilgrim decanter. The label had been printed from skillfully engraved plates, but the manufacturer's code was wrong and the paper was of a cheaper grade than the high rag content of the genuine ones; also, the green of the ink had a slight yellowish tinge that should not have been present. And the federal tax stamp had a series of perforations which revealed it to be a forgery.

He replaced the botle. In none of the other taverns he'd visited had he tasted anything other than true Old Pilgrim, not even the fairly smooth copy manufactured by the Organization. He had no idea why the outlaw distiller had made an exception in his nondistribution to local outlets, and gone ahead and supplied the New Old Lompoc House with his 'shine. But now that he had a definite lead to go on—

The overhead lights suddenly blazed on.

Flagg whirled, crouching, his hand dipping inside his jacket. He let it freeze when he saw the cocktail waitress standing in the storage room doorway. No longer wearing her costume, she was dressed now in a pair of tight corduroy pants and a striped ski jacket, and she held a small, lightweight deer rifle cradled in her hands. The muzzle was pointed straight at his belly.

She said, "I remember you," as if she were very disappointed. "You were in here earlier, but I'd never have figured you were casing the place for a burglary."

Flagg relaxed, straightening. A person who talks usually isn't inclined to shoot. "You were supposed to have gone home by now," he said.

"I live in one of the cabins out there," she told him coldly. "I couldn't sleep, so I decided to take a walk. And I saw you fooling around at the rear door."

"So you trotted back home and got your rifle," Flagg said. "Well, all right, you can put it down now."

"The hell I can."

He took a short, exploratory step forward. "Calm down," he said, and took another step. "This isn't what it looks like."

"No?"

"No. I can explain."

"Save your explaining for the sheriff."

"You're not going to call any sheriff."

"Just watch me."

"You're not, because you don't want the law nosing around here," Flagg said. "Not with this joint peddling bootleg."

"What?"

"You heard me. Bootleg; moonshine hooch."

"I heard you, but I don't believe you," she said. "That sort of thing went out with Prohibition."

Flagg, smiling wryly, moved a step closer. "Illicit liquor traffic is heavier than ever. It's a nation-wide, multi-million-dollar industry, and you're an accessory to it each time you serve a drink."

"Balls, mister, you can't—"

Flagg took two quick shuffling steps forward and jerked the rifle out of her hands. She made a small cry, her eyes widening. He backed off, angling the weapon downward. "But I can," he said.

She was frightened now. "What're you going to do?"

"That depends on you."

"Meaning?"

"Meaning it depends on how deep you're involved, and how much you'll cooperate," Flagg said. "I'm not kidding; I know for a fact the Old Pilgrim used as a house bourbon here is pure 'shine."

"Well, if it is, it's news to me."

"You're not what I call cooperating. What's your name?"

"Toni. Toni Kenyon." Nervously she brushed strands of her blonde hair back from her forehead. "But I'm not involved with anything or anybody, is that clear?"

Flagg studied her for another long moment. "Listen, Toni," he said, "I'm going to level with you. I'm probably putting my butt in a sling doing it, but I'm at a deadend otherwise."

"What are you talking about?"

"I'm a Federal agent," he said, watching her face for a reaction. Her eyebrows knitted, but that was all. No, she wasn't in on the bootlegging; he felt positive of that now.

"I'm with the Bureau of Alcohol, Tobacco and Firearms, based in Portland," Flagg continued. He took out the wallet Churlak had provided, flashed her the badge and ID card that showed him to be Special Agent Jim Harter. "Somebody is distilling and distributing large quantities of contraband liquor in these parts. It's my assignment to find out who."

She glanced at his credentials, then looked back up at him. "You've still got no right breaking in," she said, but her expression seemed to be one of relief. "So okay, you're not the regular sort of burglar, but what's all this got to do with me?"

"I need your help."

"I keep telling you, Mr Harter, I don't know a thing."

"Jim."

"Whatever you fancy, but honest, I can't help you."

"But you'll answer a few questions?"

"I'll try, Mr . . . Jim."

"How long have you been here?"

"Just over a year."

"Is the name Gino Trenotti familiar?"

"Sure. Gino worked here the last couple of months."

"That's all?"

"Well, the news said he got shot robbing an armored

car."

"Besides that. What was his job here?"

"Bartending. But he and Morley had something else cooking, some sort of private deal, I think." Toni was becoming more intrigued and less reticent. "Gino wasn't the bootlegger, was he?"

"Doubtful, but he did have underworld connections," Flagg said. "Where does Morley Ogden buy his liquor?"

"From Emerald Wholesale, in Roseburg."

"Is that his only supplier?"

"Emerald's the only distributor I've seen stop here," she said. "That is, of hard liquor. That is what you mean, isn't it?"

"Yes. Who else makes scheduled deliveries?"

"Well, Tankard brings us our beer, and Chevalier our wine." She paused, then added thoughtfully, "But they can't be the ones."

"Why?"

"Because the beer's either in kegs or bottles, and the wine's in bottles, too—and none of them look at all like a whisky-bottle."

"Smart girl. Anybody else?"

"The snack food company, and the soft-drink people. We do our own laundry, so that's out. Oh, and Tru-test Petroleum, of course. I'm afraid that's all, Jim."

Flagg frowned, rubbing his ear. "Tru-test Petroleum?"

"That's right. It's a fuel oil company."

"How often does it deliver?"

"About once a week."

"Even during the summer?"

"Now that you mention it, yes," Toni answered reflectively. "You know, I remember it struck me as a little odd, Morley ordering so much kerosene last season. It was hot, and the furnace wasn't on."

"Uh-huh. Was it pumped in, or come in drums, or what?"

"Cases. Morley said it was easier to handle that way."

"Where does he store the cases?"

"In the small boiler room off the storage room."

"Show me," Flagg told her.

They went into the storage room, with Flagg switching off the overhead lights as they left the bar. The boiler-room door was partially hidden behind some of the crates; he had missed it in the darkness earlier. It was locked, but he worked on the latch with a set of lock-picks, which he had disguised as part of a large Swiss Army knife, and soon had it open. Inside, he broke open one of the four dozen stacked cases marked *Fuel Oil—Inflammable*.

The case was filled with bottles of Old Pilgrim.

Toni stared, incredulous. "My God, you were right."

"It had to be here someplace. Now, where's Trutest?"

"In Medford," she said. "In Emmetville, actually, a little community right next to Medford. For all practical purposes, Emmetville's part of Medford.

"Where in Emmetville?"

"On Hathaway Boulevard. It's a big yard, between a cannery and a fruit-packing plant. And it's fenced."

"Guarded?"

Toni nodded. "I've never been in there, but I understand you have to have some kind of special pass to get past the gate."

Flagg rubbed his ear again. "Who owns Tru-test?"

"Vincent Burleigh."

"Do you know what he looks like?"

"Well, I'd say he was in his fifties," Toni replied. "He's a very short man, barely five feet, and he's slender—muscular but lean, except for a middle-aged paunch. His hair is gray and slicked back, he has a little mustache like the older men in movies used to have, and he's a slick dresser. Always wears expensive sport clothes. He drives a big Continental and acts like he's God's gift to women."

"Sounds like you know him pretty well."

"To look at. He comes in now and then."

"To drink or to see Ogden?"

"Both. He usually buys one and sits making noises at me, like I'm supposed to swoon at his feet. Or maybe it's the damn costume Morley makes me wear that turns him on. Anyway, then him and Morley and Gino, when he was here, all go into Morley's office, shut the door, and do whatever it is they do in there."

Flagg said, "Okay," and smiled at her. "I'm going to trust you to keep quiet about all this. "Don't betray that trust."

"You don't have to worry. When it comes to the Feds, I'm everybody's sweet little angel."

"Good," he said. "What's your cabin number?"

"Hold on, I'm not going to be *that* cooperative."

He laughed. "It's only in case I need more information."

"Well . . . It's cabin fifteen, but remember what I said."

"I'll do that. And you remember what *I* said."

When she nodded Flagg broke open her rifle and emptied it, putting the cartridges in his jacket pocket. Then he handed the rifle back to Toni, saying, "You might as well head back to your cabin now. I'll be leaving as soon as I clean up here."

"You want me to help?"

"No. It'll only take me a couple of minutes."

When Toni had gone, Flagg returned the bottle of Old Pilgrim he'd taken from one of the cases, closed the lid and then relocked the boiler-room door. There was no way he could conceal the broken hasp on the storage-room entrance, but when Morley Ogden didn't find anything missing in the morning, he might put it down to vandals.

Flagg took the tire-iron with him and stowed it in his camper. Then he began the long drive down to the Big Pine.

He would have preferred to spend the night somewhere near the Tru-test yard, sleep in the camper. But he didn't want Villareal, Lyons and Northrup to mark him as missing for the night; it was a simple matter of not wanting the left hand to know what the right hand was up to, at least not until he had determined if there were any connections between the hijackings and the bootlegging. Even if there was no connection, and the two were entirely separate problems, he doubted he would confide in anyone except Churlak. On a need-to-know basis, which was how he liked to operate, the

DynaFreight boys didn't need to know anything.

When he reached the Big Pine and parked the camper in its slot, he saw that everything was quiet. All of the cars belonging to the DynaFreight trio were present and accounted for. The matchstick he had slipped into his room's doorjamb was still in place, indicating that nobody had tried to break in while he'd been gone. But he went in cautiously anyway, with his hand on the holstered .38. The room was empty, untouched.

He reset the alarm, undressed and slid into bed. Waiting for sleep, he again mulled over all the events since the hijacking, searching for leads he might have overlooked. The more he thought, the more frustrated he became. He still felt that he'd seen or heard something significant, somewhere along the line, but whatever it was, it remained wedged in his subconscious. He was still trying to pry it free when fatigue pushed him over the edge into sleep.

TEN

Flagg slept another three hours before the alarm rang. He showered again in still colder water, dressed in a pair of dirty Levi's and a stained workshirt and left his room.

Walking to the camper, he noticed Villareal, Lyons and Northrup eating breakfast in the cafe. They saw him, too, and beckoned for him to join them, but he only waves casually in their direction and continued toward the camper.

Villareal got out of the booth and came trotting outside. "Wait!" he called, and when he had caught up to Flagg, he said: "We're ready to go anytime. What's on the agenda?"

"There's no agenda."

"Yeah, well, where're you going?"

"I've got a doctor's appointment at ten."

"You're coming right back afterwards, aren't you?"

"I don't know. Why?"

"What do you mean, why?" Villareal scowled. "You don't expect us to just sit around twiddling our thumbs, do you?"

"None of you were asked to stay here."

"I know, but—"

"You invited yourselves," Flagg said, climbing into the cab. "You know the score, and thanks to your mouth, Lyons does too. But Northrup supposedly doesn't. So do you expect me to carry all of you with me like a goddamn caravan while I'm trying to do my work?"

"Maybe not, but what do you want us to do?"

"Go back to Grants Pass," Flagg said, and started the engine.

He left Villareal standing there in the parking lot, arms stiff at his sides, mouth agape like a salmon's.

By nine-thirty, Flagg had reached Medford. He stopped at an auto supply store and bought a small assortment of mechanic's tools and a metal box to tote them in. Then he asked directions to Emmetville.

Following the route he was given, he drove west through Medford on Highway 238. As Toni had told him, Emmetville abutted the Medford line and was merely a continuation of the urban sprawl flanking the highway. Hathaway Boulevard was the first major intersection after the city limits sign; Flagg turned north on it, passed more discount stores and fast-food eateries and eventually came to a long stretch of pear orchards, canneries and fruit-packing plants.

He cruised by Tru-test and pulled in next door to it, in the wide vacant yard of Empire Packers. He parked far off to one side, got out and studied his left front wheel. Then, cursing in a loud voice, he walked up Empire Packers' long, low ramshackle building and entered the door marked *Shipping & Receiving Only*.

Since the packing season was long over, the building

was used mainly as a warehouse. Just a few workers were on the job; the clerk handling the bookwork in the office appeared pleased to see a fresh face to break the monotony. "Yes?" he asked, smiling.

"My truck broke down," Flagg told him. He gestured back toward where the camper was parked. "Front brakes seized on me."

The clerk glanced out the window and nodded sympathetically. "You can leave it there, I guess. It should be safe enough."

"I can fix it, soon as I get another brake drum," Flagg said. "If I can use your phone, I'll call around and see if I can find one."

"Be my guest."

The clerk brought out a phone directory and Flagg looked up wrecking yards in the Yellow Pages. On the second try, he located one which had a used Chevy drum and was willing to deliver it in a couple of hours. Then he thanked the clerk and went back outside.

Getting the tire-jack and iron out of camper, he raised the front end and removed the left rim. He rolled the tire aside, used the tools he'd bought to take off the brake drum. Afterward, he sat in the cab, placidly smoking his briar, and waited for Economee Auto Dismantlers & Recyclers to arrive with the replacement drum.

From time to time, in a seemingly disinterested manner, Flagg glanced at the fenced compound of Tru-test Petroleum. It was a large concern. The main entrance was some seventy-five yards to the south on Hathaway and there was a sentry-box there with a uniformed guard. The gates opened electronically, from controls inside the box. Flagg could not see much of what went on inside the compound.

During the next two hours, several dark green delivery trucks with the company name emblazoned on their doors and sides arrived and departed at regular intervals. One large diesel tanker without any markings came at twenty to eleven and left thirty minutes later. A new Continental driven by a very short man entered the Tru-test grounds at eleven-forty. There was no other traffic.

Just before noon, a pickup from Economee showed up at the packing-plant yard. Flagg paid cash for the drum, including an extra core charge so he wouldn't have to give up his original drum; he didn't want anyone, even Economee, to wonder why he'd gone to all this trouble and expense to replace a perfectly good part. He put on the other drum, replaced the tire and jacked down the front end. Tossing his tools and the old drum inside the cab, he started the engine and turned back onto Hathaway the way he'd come.

Three blocks from the intersection with Highway 238, he stopped at a Chinese restaurant and ordered a combination dinner and tea to go. While he was waiting for his food, he used the pay-phone to call Churlak collect in San Francisco. He told Churlak what he'd learned so far; and after a short discussion they agreed what he should do next, what he would need and where to pick it up.

Flagg returned to the camper, which was parked at the curb, and began eating his dinner. He had almost finished the Hui Mein when another dark green tank truck, similar to the one he'd seen earlier, passed him in the other lane and proceeded up Hathaway toward Tru-test. Flagg stayed where he was, finishing his meal.

A half hour later, the tanker came back. Flagg was ready for it. He waited until it had turned left at the intersection, then started the camper and swung out after it. The tanker continued at a good clip southwesterly along 238. The highway began climbing through foothills, looping around Timber Mountain and veering northwesterly toward Grants Pass. Flagg followed at a discreet distance.

They had travelled some twenty-five miles when the tanker turned off onto a county road in poor repair — the kind map-makers call "Unimproved, inquiry suggested." And according to the map Flagg had open on his lap, this road wandered through the middle of the Siskiyou National Forest and joined Route 46 coming from the Oregon Caves National Monument. Apparently the tanker was delivering fuel oil to a government wilderness.

Six miles along the road, however, and not yet to the government boundary, the tanker turned again. This time it was on a packed-earth road flanked by signs reading: *Private Property—Trespassers Will Be Prosecuted*.

Flagg passed by, gazing up at the private road. A couple of hundred yards along he could see two men with rifles. A third man was swinging open a heavy wooden gate to allow the tanker admittance.

Flagg followed the county road for another quarter-mile, turned around and came back again. The tanker had disappeared and the gate was closed. The men were still there.

He returned to 238 and continued on to Grants Pass.

From there he went north on Interstate 5 for another eight miles, until he reached the first rest area. It was gouged out of a deeply wooded grove, with a parking lot, a small concrete block building with rest-rooms, and a cluster of picnic tables nestled among the trees.

Pulling in at the extreme end, he used the men's room and then settled down in the camper to wait for Churlak's courier.

ELEVEN

At ten to four that afternoon, the very short man drove his new Continental out of the Tru-test yard. The guard at the gate waved, but the short man paid no attention to him.

Twenty minutes later, another of the large diesel tankers arrived at the entrance. The guard in his box nodded to the two men in the tanker cab, pushed the button that electronically controlled the gates. The gates were beginning to roll open on their tracks when a white panel truck with the words *Rite-A-Way Plumbing, Inc.* plastic-stenciled on the sides drove up in back of the tanker and honked as if impatient to get through.

The guard came out of the box, gesturing for the truck to stop where it was. The gates were closing behind the tanker as he approached the truck and looked inside. "Yeah?"

"Here to fix the john in the warehouse," Flagg said. He wore a pair of faded blue overalls and a baseball cap and was puffing on his briar pipe again.

The guard frowned. "Mr Burleigh didn't mention anything about a plumber coming in."

"Well, he called the shop less than an hour ago."

"What's the matter with the john?"

"He didn't give me any details," Flagg said, "except that it was clogged. Check with him, if you want."

"He's not here right now."

"Well, he was here an hour ago; I talked to him myself."

"He left twenty minutes ago."

"When'll he be back?"

"Not till tomorrow morning."

"Listen," Flagg said irascibly. "You see the sign on my truck? Rite-A-Way Plumbing. That's me, right-away on the job. But it's no skin off me one way or the other if I do it or not. There's an automatic service charge just for me to come out here and argue."

The guard chewed at his lower lip with indecision. "I don't know," he said. "How long will you be?"

"Now how can I tell that if I haven't seen the problem yet? This Mr. Burleigh seemed to think I ought to see about it pronto, but if you don't think so, I'll be on my way. Like I said, there's an automatic service charge—"

"Okay, okay, you made your point," the guard said. "Do you know where the main warehouse is?"

"Nope, never been here before."

"Follow the white lines until you come to a big corrugated dock along one side. Go on around to Door Five and ask for Lou. He's the one in charge there; he can tell you where the john is."

"Got it," Flagg said. "Thanks."

The guard opened the gates from inside his sentry-box and Flagg drove the panel onto the Tru-test grounds. He followed the white lines as directed and a couple of minutes later he parked in front of Door Five of the long, narrow warehouse, the roof of which he had spotted from the Empire Packers yard.

There were three of the dark green delivery trucks pulled up to the loading platform in front of other numbered doors, and a good deal of activity on the dock itself. Pallets of boxes with markings identical to those he had seen in the boiler room of the New Old Lompoc House were being stacked at intervals by two forklifts. Freight handlers were hurrying back and forth with dollies between the pallets and the trucks.

Flagg got out of the panel and opened the rear doors and took out a large tool-chest. Then he went up several wooden steps and through Door Five. A chubby man with thinning hair was writing on a clipboard. Flagg approached him and asked, "Where's Lou?"

"I'm Lou," the man answered.

"I'm here to fix the john," Flagg said.

"There's nothing wrong with it."

"Well, I got this call to come out and fix it."

Lou gave him a long appraising look. Flagg puffed disinterestedly on his pipe. Finally Lou said, "I suppose you must've been called, to get past the gate. Come on, I'll show you where it is."

Flagg followed him along the concrete floor of the warehouse past more full pallets stacked three high. At the far wall, between stacks, there was a door marked *No Admittance*. Loud vibrant sounds of machinery filtered through the door. To one side was another door marked *Rest Room*, and Lou opened that one. They went in.

"See? Nothing's wrong," Lou said.

"You can't tell without checking it."

"How long will that take?"

"What am I? Psychic?"

"Just make it quick, all right?"

Flagg opened the tool-chest, rummaged around inside and brought out a pair of groove-joint pliers and a large sponge. He used the pliers to shut off the water to the toilet, then flushed its tank empty and began soaking up the remaining water in the bowl with the sponge, which he squeezed into the basin. It was sloppy work; he managed to spray the water about, getting some of it on Lou's shoes.

"Hey, watch it," Lou snapped.

"What do you expect? This is no auditorium, you know."

"Ahh," Lou said, and went out, slamming the door.

Flagg straightened and stood at the door, listening. After a minute, he opened it and peered out. Lou had disappeared among the stacks of pallets. Flagg closed the door, locked it.

There was a window in the rear wall; he went to it and brushed some of the dust from the glass and looked out. He could see across to where the fuel pumps were located. The diesel tanker that had arrived ahead of him was parked there, and four men were standing around it. One end of a huge black petroleum hose was hooked to a bottom outlet on the first of the tanker's two reservoirs; the other end was connected to a large valve set into the concrete.

Underground tanks, Flagg thought. And then: Well, I'll be damned! He had just realized that with the hose hooked to the bottom outlet on the reservoir, they couldn't possibly be filling the tanker—they were *emptying* it. Funny. The tanker was one of Tru-test's, not a delivery vehicle from a refinery. Why would they be emptying fuel oil from one of their own trucks back into the underground tanks? Unless . . .

Unless it wasn't fuel oil.

Unless it was moonshine.

Sure, that was it. They were storing their bootleg in the underground tanks. But it made his task that much harder, Flagg realized. He had hoped to find the actual still in operation here at Tru-test; that would have made things relatively simple. Instead, they were trucking the booze in, most likely from those wild hills bordering the Siskiyou National Forest. And God only knew how far back that private dirt road went; or how many men, rifles and even traps were strung about up in there to foil raids.

Flagg listened to the machinery sounds coming through the wall and thought about the door marked *No Admittance*. With the moonshine being stored here, and distributed from here, they were obviously bottling it here too. He knew what he would discover on the other side of that door: a long, three-sided roller belt, with stainless-steel machinery along it which would fill, cap, label and stamp the bottles of "Old Pilgrim", with a direct pipeline to the storage tanks outside. But he didn't need to get a look inside there, now.

Patiently, he allowed five minutes to pass by. Then he turned on the water to the toilet again, put the pliers and sponge away. Before closing the tool-chest, he took out a ratty old gasket formed from inch-thick wax. He unlocked the door and walked through the warehouse to Door Five, where Lou was standing with his clipboard.

"Well?" Lou asked.

"I fixed it," Flagg said.

"Yeah? What was the trouble?"

Flagg held up the gasket. "The seal was shot."

Lou made a face. "I'm glad I ain't got your job."

"Sometimes I wish I didn't either," Flagg said sourly.

He went down the steps and placed the tool-chest and gasket into the rear of the panel. He drove to the front gate and the same guard came out of the sentry-box to remark, "That was fast."

"Sure," Flagg said. "Rightaway with Rite-A-Way."

The guard opened the gates. Flagg drove out, turned south on Hathaway Boulevard and stopped at the first half-decent service station he came to; he scrubbed his hands and forearms in the men's room. Then he drove through Medford and back onto Interstate Five, heading north toward that first rest area.

The sun was just a few crimson streaks on the western horizon when he reached the rest area. Shadows crowded in among the grove of trees beyond. His camper was the only vehicle in sight and there was no sign of the young courier who had delivered the truck.

He pulled in alongside the camper, shut off the motor. The cab of the camper was empty; he could see that. He waited another minute or so, but the courier didn't come out of the rest-rooms or over from the picnic area. Frowning, Flagg stepped out of the truck and knocked the dottle from his pipe. The courier was supposed to stay with the camper until he returned.

Hitches in plans usually turned out to be nothing important, but Flagg did not care to take chances. Just in case somebody other than the courier was around, perhaps hiding and watching, he walked down toward the rest-room building, surveying the picnic grounds and the grove beyond. He checked inside the men's room and then came back, scrutinizing the woods again. Then he went around to the rear of the camper and opened its tailgate door.

The man hidden inside fired a rifle point-blank.

Flagg had made sure to stay on the far side of the door when he wrenched it open. The man shot nervously, trigger-happy, but he was also quick to recover when he realized Flagg wasn't standing there in the doorway. He fired a long burst to keep Flagg from gaining the drop, opening a perforated line all along the thin aluminium siding of the camper, and then he came lunging out.

Flagg was already sprinting for the grove of trees. Only an idiot would stand and face a semi-automatic rifle with what he carried, a snub-nosed .38. The woods offered cover and were better for infighting with a pistol than with a long-barrelled rifle. At least, that was how he figured it as he pounded over the picnic grounds and dodged in among the trees.

The rifle opened up again behind him, the sound echoing dully; bullets ripped through the brush close by him. He stopped running when he reached the cover of a big-boled pine, glanced back. Through a cross-hatch of branches, he glimpsed the man leaning on the hood of the camper, the rifle butted at his shoulder. But an instant later the weapon lowered and the man began running in a zigzag across the picnic grounds. The distance and his erratic movements spoiled any chance for Flagg to use his .38.

Flagg pivoted and plunged deeper into the grove. He had gone another twenty feet when he heard the rifle again, simultaneous with the splintering crack of wood overhead. Needles showered down around him. He crushed through a thicket of briars and creepers, angled left for several more yards toward the shelter of a large boulder. The rifle cracked another time; this bullet ricocheted off the boulder. Flagg veered left and dropped into a shallow gully. He hugged the earth as still another shot sprayed dirt over his neck.

Then there was stillness.

Flagg lay there, catching his breath, not liking the quiet. This was not one of those lush, statuesque forests. This was a northern flood-plain forest, whose trees were generally sparse and spindly and not much good at filtering out what light there was left. The ground was a jagged, scalloped washboard of gnarled scrub, thorn patches, rotting logs and branches and loose stone and boulders. A target could be silhouetted a thirty yards, but could just as readily be standing motionless behind a nearby trunk or poised on the other side of the same. Or lying in a ditch-sized gully like this one that was impossible to spot until you fell into it.

The silence stretched on. The forest seemed to grow increasingly hushed, oppressive, like the atmosphere in a cemetery. Flagg felt very alone, very vulnerable.

Finally he eased his head up over the rim of the gully. There was no shot. Either the man had missed seeing him in the shadowy light, or he was holding off while some traveller parked at the rest area. Flagg didn't think the shooter had left. He'd come here to commit murder and the odds were that he'd want to stick around until he completed the job.

Flagg lowered himself flat, inched to his right along the gully. He made fifteen yards in almost as many minutes. Then the gully ended at a large outcropping of rock and there was no way to pass around it, not with a briar patch on one side and the crumbling crust of a log on the other. He reached out and shinnied himself up onto the bare face of the rock.

There was a flash and a bullet nicked the stone next to his shoulder. He vaulted over the top and hit the underbrush rolling, then dove behind another boulder a few feet beyond that.

He leaned against the rock, breathing harshly. But he couldn't hide behind the boulder forever and the shooter knew it as well as he did. He tried to figure how the man would anticipate his movements. Logically, Flagg would attempt either to break for the rest area, where there was transportation, or to bury himself further back in the woods. So Flagg did neither of those things. He slid from the protection of the boulder and began to advance in the direction of the last shot.

He eased his way across the ground on elbows and knees, testing each foot of ground, avoiding any slight obstacle that had to be scaled or might produce noise. He estimated the shot had come twenty-five to thirty yards diagonally to his right and, like it or not, he recognized the fact that his only real chance was to get close to the shooter. But if the man had also switched positions by now . . .

Suddenly there was movement ahead and to one side and Flagg saw the man. He was only a few yards away, a stocky dark outline gliding among the trees.

Flagg pressed low, holding his breath, his hand tight around the .38. The man took his own sweet time about coming to roost again, but at least he hadn't moved out of handgun range. Sweat beaded Flagg's forehead, stinging his eyes, threatening to blur his vision; he rubbed it away. He's lost me, Flagg thought; he's not sure where I am, how close I am, and he's worried.

The shooter finally stopped moving, hunkered down alongside a tree and scanned the area. Flagg ducked down out of sight. Just as he raised his head again, something—a small animal of some kind—made an unexpected noise in the brush on the other side of the tree where the man was concealed. It startled the shooter, made him lever up and twist around in surprise, so that he was crouched in the open with his backside in Flagg's direction. He fired into the brush where the animal was.

Flagg shot him twice.

The man folded as if hinged and collapsed on his rifle. Flagg ran toward him, revolver at the ready in case there was any trickery. But the most the shooter could do was to roll over off the rifle, his face contorted with pain.

Flagg hunkered beside him. "Who sent you?"

The man coughed; blood came from his mouth and nostrils. He gasped, trying to breathe.

"Who sent you?"

The man started to cough again and then to choke.

He died that way, choking spasmodically, his back arched.

Flagg gave the body a swift but thorough search. He found a comb, a pocket-knife, a crumpled pack of Marlboros and an old Zippo lighter, but nothing of consequence. He was not surprised. He recognized the dead man as one of the hijackers, the one who had hidden in the sleeper compartment, and thus enough of a pro not to carry identification.

Still, that left a bunch of unanswered questions. Such as who had set up the ambush, and how this one had known where to waylay Flagg. It definitely had not been all the doing of the dead hijacker; there weren't any keys, and there'd been no other car parked in the rest area, which indicated somebody else had dropped the man off here.

Flagg picked up the rifle, a .30-06 Remington 742A, and walked out of the grove. The rear door of the camper was still wide open. He glanced inside. Churlak's young courier was huddled up against the front wall, his mouth slack, eyes startled, his blood soaking the front of his shirt and puddling on the floor.

Flagg put the rifle on the front seat of the cab, went over to the plumbing truck and scrounged around among the tools and fittings. He returned to the camper with an arm-load of work rags and a short-handled spade used for sewer repairs. Then he climbed into the rear, dragged the courier toward the door and laid the rags over the bloodstains. Backing out, he checked the courier and removed his wallet and other personal possessions and the keys to the camper. He hefted the dead man across his shoulder, caught up the shovel with his left hand, struggled across the picnic grounds and through the trees. He dumped the body alongside that of the hijacker.

He set to work digging a common grave. The ground was hard; he used the spade as a pick as much as he did as a shovel. When he had gouged out a three-foot-deep trench, he rolled both bodies into it, covered them with soil and arranged the ground cover so that it appeared as natural and undisturbed as possible.

Wearily he returned to the rest area for the last time. He was stained with blood now, most of it along his right shoulder and the saddle of his back; he changed out of the plumber's coveralls and baseball cap, back into Levi's and workshirt he'd left in the rear of the camper. Then he mopped up the last of the blood, dumped the soggy rags, the stained clothing and the spade inside the plumbing truck. He locked up the panel and hid the keys inside the engine's air cleaner.

He drove the camper out of the rest area, still heading north. At the first exit where he could turn around, he stopped at a service station and phoned Churlak with the news.

Churlak didn't like it worth a damn. But then, neither did Flagg.

TWELVE

It was after eight when Flagg wheeled the camper into the parking lot of the New Old Lompoc House.

The lot was half-full and so was the tavern's interior. The barn-like room seemed even darker tonight, except for the musicians' dais at the far end. A pair of pale spotlights bathed that, the three-piece country-and-western combo that was playing on it, and a singer in a white-spangled outfit who was giving a poor imitation of Kenny Rogers.

Flagg stood just inside the door, peering through a cigarette haze at the bar. Morley Ogden wasn't behind it; the bartender was somebody Flagg had never seen before. But Toni was there, waiting on tables off to one side. He waited until she turned toward the bar and he was able to catch her eye. Then he found an empty table that wasn't too near any of the other customers and sat down.

Toni paused at the bar long enough to give the bartender a drink order and was standing at Flagg's table ten seconds later. "Hi, Jim," she said. "I didn't expect to see you again so soon."

"I didn't expect to be here again so soon. Where's

Ogden tonight?"

"He's here. In his office." There was a hint of excitement in her eyes; she bent closer and lowered her voice an octave. "Burleigh's with him."

"Just the two of them?"

"Yes."

"How long have they been in there?"

"About ten minutes."

"You wouldn't have any idea what they're talking about?"

"No. I wanted to sneak over and listen, but it's just too crowded in here."

"Did Burleigh act any different tonight?" Flagg asked. "Seem nervous, agitated, anything like that?"

"Not that I noticed."

"How about Ogden?"

"Same answer. Why do you ask?"

"Federal business. You don't want to know."

"No," Toni said, "I guess I don't."

She was still leaning toward him and, with that skimpy sateen costume she wore, Flagg had a good view of the shadowed hollow between her breasts and a lot of creamy white flesh on either side. Some other time he might have been interested. Not now.

He said, "Can you get off for a few minutes?"

"I guess I can take a short break. Why?"

"I want to talk to you. Not like this; in private."

"My cabin?"

"That's good," Flagg said. "But not right away. After Burleigh and Ogden come out. And after you see me leave—make it about ten minutes."

Toni nodded. "Go on around to the back and I'll let

you in there. You remember the number?"

"I remember it," Flagg said.

"Do you want me to bring you anything? A drink?"

"Just a beer."

She moved off. Flagg sat watching the closed door to Ogden's office, trying not to listen to the twangy lyrics coming out of the Kenny Rogers imitation. His mind kept turning over possibilities. He still hadn't put much of it together yet, but he was getting close—he could feel that much.

He spent twenty minutes nursing the beer Toni brought. Then the door to Ogden's office opened and Burleigh and the ex-boxer came out and headed for the bar. Ogden ducked under the swing bar at the end and the dapper owner of Tru-test took a stool facing him.

Flagg got up and wandered over to the cigarette machine that was positioned less than ten feet from where the two men were. He pretended to be debating over which brand he intended to buy while he studied them. Ogden was the first to look in his direction; the fleshy face showed neither recognition nor surprise. And all Flagg got from Burleigh was a disinterested glance.

He went back to his table and finished his beer. Another ten minutes passed while Burleigh and Ogden had a drink together; then the little man slid off his stool. When Flagg was certain Burleigh was getting ready to leave, not just going off to the can, he shoved up and went straight to the door. Outside, he stood half-facing the door and was packing his pipe from his leather tobacco-pouch when Burleigh came out.

But nothing happened this time, either. Burleigh

glanced at him again on his way by, but only in a cursory way, and then went straight to his big Continental. Less than a minute later, the Lincoln's taillights were disappearing on the road out of Sweetweed.

Flagg went to the camper, took a road map of the area from the glove compartment and slipped it into his jacket pocket. Then he walked slowly to where the tourist cabins were. Number fifteen was the last one in the curving line of them, farthest from the highway and almost directly behind the tavern. It had green shutters and an old, rusty-framed swing in one corner of its narrow porch. Flagg ducked around behind it and stood in the shadows near the back door.

Toni opened up for him twelve minutes later. Inside, the cabin was furnished spartanly, but it was clean and had a comfortable, lived-in look. Flagg wondered why an attractive woman like her would want to live alone like this, out here in the middle of nowhere. But not enough to pursue it right now. Maybe he'd ask her if he saw her again.

"I can only stay ten minutes," she said. "Otherwise, Morley'll send somebody after me."

"Ten minutes is enough. How well do you know this area?"

"Pretty well, I guess. I grew up in Emmetville."

"How about the Siskiyou National Forest? Are you familiar with that part?"

"More or less," she said, frowning.

Flagg took the road map out of his pocket and spread it open on the kitchen table. He traced the road that wandered through the Siskiyou wilderness, made a mark with his fingernail at the approximate spot where the Tru-test tanker he'd followed had turned up the packed-earth road. That road wasn't on the map, which meant that it had been privately built.

"There's a dirt road about here," he said to Toni, indicating the fingernail mark. "You have any idea where it leads?"

Her brow remained furrowed as she worked her memory. "I think I know the one you mean. If I do, it leads to an old abandoned mine of some sort."

"Anything else in the area?"

"Just woodland."

"Tell me about this mine."

"I don't know much about it. I've never been up there. I think for a while it was turned into a gravel pit—some special kind of gravel used in making concrete or something. But even the quarry was abandoned about ten years ago. I seem to remember somebody telling me that a lot of gravel was taken out of the base of the hill, so that the pit almost reached the main mine-shaft."

"So it's still abandoned, as far as you know?"

"Well, I heard that somebody bought the property and was going to reactivate the quarry," Toni said. "But I don't know if that's happened yet or not."

"Is there any other way to reach the mine, except for that one dirt road?"

"The road itself only goes as far as the gravel-pit. There's an old logging road, or what's left of it, around on the other side of the mine. There's an auxiliary tunnel on that side and some ore tracks leading out of it and down to the logging road; I've seen them, one day when a . . . friend and I were out hiking. I guess they used to run ore down the hill to trucks or wagons on the logging road—maybe because the auxiliary tunnel is higher up, where the mine tower is, and they couldn't get the ore out through the regular entrance below."

"How about foot trails in the vicinity?" Flagg asked.

"None that you could follow for very long." Toni paused. "Do you think that's where the moonshine is being made?"

Flagg shrugged. "I'm not sure yet," he said. "How do I find that logging road?"

"Follow the county road past where the mine road intersects. About five miles farther along, there's a little creek with the remains of a wooden bridge across it— just a few rotting timbers. The logging road is just beyond those timbers, on the far side of the creek."

"So I can't take a car up there?"

"No. The road's too overgrown after all these years. You'll have to walk." She paused again. "But you're not going up to the mine alone, are you?" she asked, and there was something in her voice that might have been concern.

Flagg gave her a lopsided smile. "Don't worry about me," he said. "A couple more questions, and you can go back to work."

"Go ahead," she said solemnly.

"Has either Ogden or Burleigh ever mentioned DynaFreight when you were around?"

"DynaFreight," she said, as if testing the word. "No, I don't think so. What's that?"

"A trucking line out of Grants Pass. You've never heard of it?"

"It doesn't ring any bells."

"How about the name Villareal?"

"No, I've never heard that one, either."

"Northrup?"

She shook her head.

"Ben Lyons?"

Another headshake. "Who are all those people?"

"I wish I knew just who they were," Flagg said. "When Trenotti was alive and working here, did he know Burleigh pretty well too?"

"Well, he used to go into Morley's office with the two of them sometimes, so I guess he did. Do you think he was mixed up in the bootlegging scheme, same as Morley?"

"He probably was," Flagg said. And thought that maybe it had worked out for the best when Trenotti was killed in the abortive armored-car heist. The Organization didn't take kindly to being doublecrossed by people it bankrolled and offered protection to, even if it was in a separate kind of deal. You played square with the Organization, down the line, and the Organization played square with you; otherwise you wouldn't be around very long. Churlak and the other top men believed in non-violence these days, but that didn't mean they were above setting an example or two. Trenotti, if he'd lived, would probably have been one of those set examples.

Not that Flagg himself would have had anything to do with that. He didn't know much about that end of the Organization's business; he had never hired out for a hit and he never would. He was a troubleshooter, a kind of detective—not an assassin.

Toni said, "Is there anything else?"

"I don't think so. Not for now, anyway. You'd better get on back."

"All right." She hesitated, then put a hand gently on his arm. "Jim, will I see you again?"

"Maybe," he said. "You never know."

"If you . . . need me, I'll be here."

He thought that there might be an invitation in her voice, that she might have changed her mind about cooperating with him in other ways, too. He smiled at her again. "Thanks, I'll remember that," he said. "Take care of yourself, Toni."

"You, too."

He slipped out through the back door and shut it quietly behind him. He waited alongside the cabin until she had come out the front way and gone back across to the tavern. There was nobody else on the grounds when he made his way to where he'd parked the camper. He drove out of the lot and headed south again, to pack it in for another night at the Big Pine Cafe.

On the way he did some more brooding, just as he had on the drive from the rest area to Sweetweed. Two questions were still uppermost in his mind. One was: How had the hijacker known where the courier was waiting with the camper? Flagg hadn't been followed out there, when he went to make the exchange for the plumbing truck; and unless there was some sort of leak at Churlak's end, which seemed unlikely, nobody could have followed the courier. It could have been a chance thing—the hijacker out scouting around for Flagg; but he didn't like that explanation because it was coincidental and because it was too amateurish. Whatever else the hijackers might be, they were pros. And the same went for whoever was pulling their strings.

And that was the second question that kept bothering him: Who had ordered the hit? It didn't make sense that the hijacker had done it on his own initiative. If he was part of some independent outfit, how could he possibly have known who Flagg was? No, it figured he was a hireling, acting on orders, and that narrowed the field down to Burleigh, Morley Ogden or one of the DynaFreight trio. There had to be a connection between the hijackings and Burleigh's Tru-test operation; he was convinced of that, now.

If Ogden had ordered the hit, or was aware of it, Flagg had reasoned a "dead man" walking into the New Old Lompoc House tonight would be bound to shake him up, and visibly. That was one of the reasons why he'd headed for Sweetweed right after calling Churlak. Only Ogden hadn't turned a hair when he saw Flagg. And neither had Burleigh. Either the two of them were right up there with Burton and Olivier as actors, or they really didn't know who Flagg was and hadn't ordered the hit. If that was so, he was left with Lyons, Villareal, or Northrup—and the hijackings would *have* to be an inside job. More and more, it looked to be shaping up that way.

So he was going to have to concentrate his investigation on that end of things, he decided. And he'd find out which of them it was, sooner or later. He had a personal stake in the matter now, and that made him a bulldog: He wouldn't let go until he'd taken a hell of a bite out of somebody's ass.

Nobody tried to kill Flagg and got away with it. Nobody.

THIRTEEN

Flagg was up at eight a.m., stiff and sore from his shootout in the woods, half-groggy from lack of sleep. As tired as he'd been when he got back to the Big Pine last night, or rather early this morning, he hadn't been able to get to sleep until well after three o'clock. He would doze for a few minutes, then snap fitfully awake with his mind clear and alert. He had too many complications rattling around inside his head—and the significant fact that was wedged in his subconscious kept needling at him, like a splinter under a fingernail.

He padded naked into the bathroom and climbed under his third cold shower in as many mornings. After a minute or so, he twisted the knobs to regulate the spray to hot. But nothing came out of the shower head except water that felt even colder. It was like standing under a spray of ice water . . .

Ice, he thought.

Christ, that's it—*ice*.

Abruptly, the memory fragment had dislodged itself and he was remembering the freshly used set of chains, still encrusted with ice, that had been in the bed of the hijackers' green pickup truck. And he was also remembering the messenger who had brought the camper telling him it was equipped with chains; but he hadn't needed them on his trips back and forth across the Oregon-California border because it hadn't been snowing at these lower elevations . . .

Flagg toweled himself dry, made a quick job of dressing in a shirt and a pair of slacks and caught up the telephone. He called the weather bureaus in Redding and Grants Pass and triple-checked with the road reporter at the Highway Patrol substation in Yreka. He learned that the recent two-day storm had dumped snow intermittently on its way down from Canada, and while most of the immediate area had received torrential rain, there was one section of the Klamath Mountains which had had blizzard conditions. More importantly, Highway 32 through that area had required chains right up until the morning he'd been hijacked —the only road in this entire area that had required them.

Flagg strapped on his .38 in its clamshell holster—he had taken the time to reload it before going to bed last night and had slept with the gun under his pillow—and slipped into his jacket. Then he went out into the cold morning air.

The parking slots in front of the cabins which Villareal and Lyons had occupied were empty and had been when he'd arrived back at the Big Pine last night. Only Northrup's wheels were still there. Flagg detoured over to Northrup's unit and knocked on the door. The DynaFreight dispatcher opened fifteen seconds later, fully dressed and freshly shaved.

He didn't seem surprised to see Flagg standing there.

His expression was bland—carefully so, Flagg thought—except for a mild curiosity. "Hello, Scofield," he said.

"Northrup. I'm looking for Mr Villareal."

"He went back to Grants Pass yesterday. Said to tell you that if you asked for him."

"How about Mr Lyons?"

"Same thing. I'm going myself after breakfast."

"How come you didn't leave yesterday too?"

"I thought maybe something might break here. Mr Villareal didn't seem to mind."

But I'll bet Lyons did, Flagg thought. He said, "Well I suppose I'll be heading back myself, pretty soon. My head's better now."

"Glad to hear it," Northrup said. There was no expression in his voice, either. "You want me to assign you a run for tomorrow?"

Even if he's not mixed up in the hijackings, Flagg thought, he's got to know I'm something more than just a truck driver. He'd have to be blind and stupid not to, and he's neither one. So why hasn't he said anything? And what's his real reason for staying on here an extra day? What's *his* angle, if it's not knocking over DynaFreight trucks?

"Better hold off until I talk to Mr Villareal," Flagg said. "I might not be going to Grants Pass until later in the day; I've got to check in with the Highway Patrol this morning. They've got some mug-shots they want me to look at. They think they might have a make on one of the hijackers."

"Oh? Which one?"

"The one that was hiding in my sleeper compartment."

Northrup didn't react to that, either. If he knew the hijacker, had sent him out after Flagg yesterday, it didn't seem to bother him that the man might be identified. Either that, or he suspected Flagg was running a bluff.

"I hope you can identify him," Northrup said. "Give us a call in Grants Pass, if you do."

"I'll do that."

"Is there any message you want me to give to Mr Villareal? Or Mr Lyons?"

"No. Just tell them I'll see them later."

Flagg left him and crossed to the cafe, where he ordered black coffee and a couple of danishes to go. Northrup came in while he was waiting, nodded to him as he passed, but didn't pause or say anything; he sat in a booth near the back, facing toward the entrance, and buried his nose in a menu.

A cool one, all right, Flagg thought. Too damned cool.

It was after nine by the time he collected his breakfast and put the camper back on the road. He ate and drank as he drove, stopped once to refuel and was on Highway 32 before half past ten.

The highway ran between Yreka on U.S. 99, and the Pacific Ocean—a corkscrew of a road passing over 8000-foot elevations. Seventy-five miles to the south was another highway connecting Redding to the coast, and double that distance to the north was Highway 199, between Grants Pass and Crescent City. It *had* to be Route 32 that he wanted; the hijackers had either come from one of the towns along it, or from farther back in the mountains where summer cabins nestled. Otherwise, that set of chains in the pickup's bed would not have been caked with ice.

Chain requirements were no longer in effect on Highway 32. But at the 3500-foot level, flakes of snow drifted down out of an overcast sky; it looked like there might be a flurry later on. The air was bitter cold and Flagg put the heater on high to keep his feet and hands warm.

He watched the snow-banked shoulders of the road as he drove. He knew the hijackers had used a truck either of the same size or larger than the cab-over he'd been driving, owing to the abandonment of the two previous DynaFreight diesels and, by this time, of his rig as well. The hijackers' truck would have left a set of tire tracks wide and deep if it turned off anywhere, since secondary roads were seldom travelled in the winter and were mostly covered with virgin snow.

He checked the towns of Silverpeak and Lovelock in passing, but no one at the places he stopped remembered either seeing or hearing of a large truck in the vicinity. He stopped at Fort Rock to order another cup of coffee to go. More snowflakes were drifting down when he came out and the wind had increased; but the sky didn't look dark enough or restless enough for any major storm activity. Light flurries were about the worst he could expect during the afternoon.

Five miles past Fort Rock, his theory paid off.

A developer had opened a flat meadow for vacation cabin sites. The field was under drifts of snow, but there was a large billboard by the entrance which guaranteed that the access roads to Spruce Hills were always open.

The developer appeared to be true to his word; the main tract road was clear, with less than two inches of frozen snow on its surface. And part of that white veneer had been flattened and compressed by wide, double-wheel tires passing over it.

Flagg swung the camper off Highway 32 and followed the tracks. The tract road passed a number of darkened, deserted A-frame cottages, and the tire marks led further inland, up a steep grade and then down into a small valley. He braked to a stop at the crest of the grade.

Below, less than a quarter mile distant, were two A-frames set in a thick half-moon of blue spruce. Through the thin snowfall, he could see that the nearest one was empty-looking, with snow piled all around it; a large van with a dented aluminium trailer was backed up alongside, under a canvas shelter. But smoke squirrel-tailed out of the stone chimney on the second cottage, and the walk in front of that one had been cleared. A four-door sedan that Flagg didn't recognize, and a familiar green pickup, were parked in a V just off the road.

He'd found the other hijackers, all right, and maybe the stolen goods along with them.

And in a little while, one way or another, he'd know the name of the bastard who had tried to write his name on the nose of a bullet.

FOURTEEN

Flagg sat for a moment, debating. Then he put the camper in reverse and backed to the nearest branch road. He drove along that for a short distance, pulled off into the driveway of a darkened cottage and cut off engine and headlights.

He got out, opened up the rear doors. In one of the interior cabinets he found a pair of binoculars in a leather case. He unpacked them and looped the glasses around his neck on their carry strap. Then he locked the camper and went around behind the cottage, to where a long slope paralleled the road.

The snow on the slope was solidly frozen and Flagg had little difficulty making his way to the crest. From there, he could see the two A-frames below. He squatted next to one of the scattered, white-mantled spruces and scanned the buildings through the binoculars. The light snowfall didn't interfere with his vision; he had a clear view of both the A-frames and the surrounding terrain. There was no sign of activity anywhere down there.

He put the binoculars back in their case and began to make his way down into the little valley. He moved cautiously, using the spruce trees for cover whenever he could and keeping well to the rear of the cabins in a diagonal trajectory. Ten minutes later he was crouched in the protective shelter of the evergreens less than fifteen yards from the rear of the nearest of the A-frames.

He heard nothing out of the ordinary, saw nothing except for the fluttering snowflakes. After another minute or so, he straightened and ran to the rear wall of the near building. He leaned against the rough boarding next to the its single rear window, listening.

Silence.

The panes of window glass were rimed with snow; Flagg used his gloved hand to clear a circle. There were muslin curtains drawn inside, though not fitted completely together, and enough of a gap remained to let him see into the darkened interior. He was able to make out a stack of cordwood against one wall—and the dark squarish outlines of several crates, stacked side by side and on top of one another.

Flagg looked at the window catch and decided he could jimmy it with a minimum of noise. He got out his Swiss Army knife and used one blade, and then another, and he had the window sliding slowly upward less than two minutes later.

He swung up and over the sill, lowered himself to the floor inside. He stood listening again, his muscles corded. No sounds anywhere. However many men there were in the immediate vicinity, they all figured to be in the second A-frame.

He closed the window, switched on his pocket flash and let the beam probe the various crates stacked on the otherwise bare floor. The markings indicated that they were full of small furnishings, baby cribs and other items. None of the crates showed the dummy markings that identified the stolen mash cookers, copper tubing and other paraphernalia that had been destined for the Organization's bootleg factory up north.

Which meant that the hijackers were either storing the equipment somewhere else, or they'd already disposed of it. He liked the second explanation much more than the first. The obvious place for them to have disposed of the cookers was Burleigh's outlaw still, and if that was what had happened, then it not only cleared up the hijackings but confirmed a tie between somebody at DynaFreight and Burleigh's Tru-test operation—somebody who was doublecrossing the Organization in a hell of a lot worse way than Gino Trenotti had, and whose death-warrant was assured as a result. The thefts of the furniture and the baby cribs were nothing more than red herrings; the hijackers had been after the bootleg equipment and nothing else, and everything else had been smoke screen to cover the traitor....

He was starting for the window again when he heard the key scrape in the front door lock.

Quickly, he switched off the flash. The key scraped again. Flagg moved behind one of the crates, blending with its shadows. A triangle of light appeared on the floor inside as the door was opened and then vanished as the door was closed again. An overhead light clicked on, flooding the room with pale illumination from a pair of naked ceiling bulbs.

Flagg tensed, waiting. A single set of footsteps

advanced across the room, moving in unbroken cadence; whoever it was seemed not to suspect anything wrong.

A booted leg appeared in Flagg's vision. He levered up in that same instant with his right arm hooked into a stiff plane, out and away from his body, the fingers rigidly extended. He stepped straight into the advancing man and jammed his stiffened fingers into the relaxed area under the wishbone, pulling the force somewhat so as not to rupture the man's heart. There was a surprised and agonized explosion of breath and the man went down as if he had run headlong into a wall. Flagg caught him before he hit the floor, propped him up against the nearest crate. When he got a good look at him he saw that it was the man who had driven the green pickup during the hijacking of Flagg's rig.

Flagg searched him; he wasn't carrying a weapon. Then he went over to the window, opened it again and scraped a handful of snow off the sill. He rubbed it over the hijacker's slack features, let some of it trickle inside the collar of the heavy fur parka the man wore. After a time, the hijacker began to moan softly and his eyes fluttered open.

Flagg had the .38 Special in his right hand; he pointed the muzzle at the man's left eye and said, "Quiet, now. Nice and quiet."

The hijacker blinked, focussing on the gun, and then blinked again and squinted past it at Flagg's face. In his eyes was a mixture of fear and bravado.

"How many men here besides yourself?" Flagg asked him.

"Go screw yourself."

"That's not the right answer. How many men here?"

"Go screw yourself."

Flagg scraped the barrel of the .38 along the man's cheek, poked it inside the left ear—not gently. Then he thumbed back the hammer. "This is the last time I ask you. How many others here besides you?"

Fear-tightened lips worked for several seconds before words came. Then, "Two."

"What are they doing?"

"Eating lunch."

"Are they armed?"

"No."

"Where are all the guns?"

"In a cabinet in the front room."

"Locked?"

"No."

"But closed up?"

"Yeah."

"And *all* the guns are in there?"

"All of them, yeah."

"You'd better not be lying," Flagg said. "If you are, you'll be the first one I shoot."

"I'm not lying."

"Why did you come out here?"

"To get some firewood."

"All right," Flagg said. "No more questions. You can get on your feet."

He took the muzzle of the .38 out of the hijacker's ear, straightened up. The man stood painfully, his right hand pressed to the area under his wishbone. Flagg prodded him to the door. Pausing there, he asked, "Can they see this A-frame from where they're eating?"

"No. The window is curtained."

"Move out," Flagg said.

They went out into the snow-packed area fronting the two cabins, following a cleared path across to the front door. When they got there Flagg jabbed the .38 into the man's back and breathed against his ear, "Open it. And if you say or do anything afterward, you're a dead man."

The hijacker reached out and clicked the door open. Flagg shoved him forward; the door flew inward and slammed against the inside wall, making a sharp echoing crack like that of a rifle shot. The hijacker went stumbling onto his knees in the middle of the room.

Flagg stood framed in the doorway with the .38 sweeping the interior. "As you were," he said.

The two men sitting at the table drawn up near the fireplace were shock-frozen, their hands in plain sight. The one on the left was the last of the hijacking team; but it was the one on the right, whose face was blanched a sickly white, that Flagg was most interested in.

He said, "Hello, Lyons. Hello, you son of a bitch."

FIFTEEN

Ben Lyons came out of his chair. His eyes no longer carried their amused look and when he spoke his normally modulated voice had a cracking edge. He said, "Listen . . . listen, Flagg, I can explain this, I can explain . . ."

"Sure you can, Ben" Flagg said. He glanced around the well-furnished room, noting the closed gun-cabinet. "Nice place you've got here. It *is* yours, isn't it?"

"Flagg, for Christ's sake . . ."

"Lucky thing I caught you home," Flagg said. "It makes things much simpler. How'd you get here, Ben? I didn't see your car. One of the boys pick you up someplace?"

Lyons's shoulders sagged. There was no bravado left in him; it had all drained away fast, just as it had drained out of the hijacker when Flagg put the .38 in his ear. He was finished now and he was smart enough to know it.

"Why'd you come up here today, Ben? To make sure everything was running smoothly? Or to find out how come your errand boy didn't blow me away yesterday?"

"No, you got it all wrong. I didn't have anything to do with that."

"Then how come you know about it?"

Lyons made a gesture at the other two. "They told me about it when I got here. Phil went after you on his own, Flagg—"

"You lying bastard," the hijacker on the floor said. He shoved up onto his feet. "You're not going to squeeze out of this and leave us holding the bag."

"Shut up, Ed."

"Go screw yourself," Ed said. It seemed to be his favourite expression. "I'm through taking orders from you."

Flagg said, "Both of you shut up. You take orders from me from now on." He made a gesture with the .38. "Where's the shipment of mash cookers, Ben?"

Lyons wet his lips.

"Well, Ben?"

"Flagg, listen, can't we make a deal?"

"No deals."

Lyons's eyes searched Flagg's face, looking for an opening, an out, and finding none at all. His gaze dipped to the gun and Flagg let his finger whiten on the trigger. Lyons took a half-stumbling step backward, putting up his right hand with the palm outward as if to ward off a bullet. Flagg felt a cut of disgust. The man was a coward as well as a fool and a traitor; he deserved whatever happened to him.

"Jesus, Flagg," he said in a quivering voice, "take it easy, will you? I'll tell you what you want to know. I'll tell you!"

"Bastard," the man named Ed said. "Lousy bastard."

The other hijacker's hands were clenched at his sides. He didn't say anything—hadn't spoken the whole time but when he looked at Lyons, his face was murderous.

"So talk to me, Ben" Flagg said. "Where's the shipment of mash cookers?"

"Gone, most of it. Already delivered."

"Except for how much?"

"Six crates."

"Where are they?"

"Here," Lyons said, and indicated a closed and barred door on the opposite side of the room. "In the storeroom."

"Where was the rest of it delivered?"

"To a man named Burleigh. He owns a petroleum outfit in Emmetville—"

"I know all about that. He's the outlaw distiller the Organization's been after, right?"

"Yes."

"Are you mixed up in his bootlegging scam, too?"

"No. I swear it, no!"

"But you know all about it."

"I knew Burleigh a long time ago, up in Portland. I didn't find out he was running the 'shine operation until about a month ago, when he came to see me. He'd found out the Organization was going to ship a load of equipment up north—"

"How did he find out?"

"Gino Trenotti told him."

"And how did Trenotti find it out?"

"He heard about it in Frisco," Lyons said. "Somebody must have leaked it to him by accident while he was arranging to bankroll that armored-car heist that got him killed."

"Okay. Go on."

"Burleigh knew I needed money for a big real-estate deal that's opening up in Medford." A flicker of greed showed in Lyons' eyes. "Flagg, it's a deal that could have made me rich—I mean *rich*. But I didn't have the capital. That's why I let Burleigh talk me into hijacking the load of cookers. He promised to finance the real-estate deal for me."

"So you brought in these two and the other one—"

"We didn't know it was Organization trucks we'd be knocking over," Ed said. "You got to believe that. If we'd known it, we'd have steered clear of the whole thing."

Flagg ignored him. He said to Lyons, "You brought in your boys and had them hijack the load of furniture as a red herring. And when you found out about me coming in undercover, you ordered the hijacking of my rig—another red herring, strictly for my benefit. That the way it was, Ben?"

"Yes."

"Only I started to get too close to the truth, and you got nervous and panicked and sent that hotshot after me yesterday."

"It was a stupid thing to do, I know that," Lyons said. His voice quivered again. "But I was scared, I didn't know what else to do. I was in so deep already . . ."

"How did he know where to find my camper, so he could set up the ambush?"

"Is that what happened?—he tried to ambush you? All I know is that Burleigh's guards spotted you when you drove past the private road that leads to the outlaw still; they thought you might've followed the tanker from Tru-test. One of them had binoculars and he got your license number and the camper's description, and passed the information on to Burleigh. Burleigh got in touch with me, to see if I knew who you might be. I knew it was you and that you were getting close. But I didn't tell Burleigh that; instead I called Phil "—meaning the dead hijacker—"and he came straight up to Grants Pass to look for you. He must have spotted you coming through."

That made sense. Flagg had gone through Grants Pass both ways—driving the camper to the rest area, driving the plumbing truck back down to Tru-test. The hijacker could have spotted him, all right. And either followed him up to the rest area, or, if he'd seen him in the plumbing truck, gone searching for the camper and found it that way.

"Flagg," Lyons said fearfully, "what happened to Phil? Did you kill him?"

"Yeah, I killed him."

"But you're not going to kill *me*, are you? You're not going to murder all three of us?"

Flagg didn't say anything.

"Flagg? You're not, are you?"

"What do you think?"

"You *can't* kill us! For the love of God—"

"Stop being melodramatic," Flagg told him. "Things aren't done that way nowadays. At least not by me." He smiled faintly. "You were a damned fool to cross the Organization, Ben. I don't care how rich that real-estate deal would have made you. Nobody crosses the Organization and gets away with it."

"I've got a good record!" Lyons pleaded. "I . . . I just lost my head. Give me a break, will you?"

"That's not my department, either."

Lyons subsided, still whimpering. He looked old and haggard, a deflated, hollow man whose one big gamble had blown up in his face.

Flagg backed over to the storeroom door, not taking his eyes off Lyons and the two hijackers. He reached behind him, lifted the crossbar off and pulled the door open wide; then he moved away from it, to where he could see inside the storeroom. It was little more than a cubicle, barren except for some boxes of foodstuff and six crates marked with the words *Machine Tools*. He noted that there were no windows and that the door was constructed of solid redwood.

He said, "Into the storeroom, all of you."

They obeyed, the two hijackers sullen, Lyons still fearful. Flagg ordered them to pick up one of the crates, had them carry it outside and put it into the bed of the green pickup. They transferred the other five crates the same way. Then he herded them back inside, into the storeroom again.

Lyons started in last, but Flagg said, "Not you, Ben. You go on over and stand against the wall where I can see you."

When Lyons turned, naked terror crawled in his eyes. But he did what he was told.

Flagg said to the two hijackers, "What I'm going to do now is lock the two of you in here and call the

Highway Patrol anonymously, with a tip on where they can find the men who've been doing the DynaFreight hijackings. All the goods are in the other A-frame, and the van and the pickup will be nearby. That's all the evidence they'll need."

The two men watched him silently.

"You'll get sent up for it," Flagg said, "but if you keep your mouths shut about the DynaFreight operation, and the boot-legging, and all the rest of it, you'll be out in a few years, free and clear. If you don't keep your mouths shut, the Organization will see to it that you spend a lot more years in the jug."

"We never heard of any Organization, mister," the one named Ed said. "We're not as dumb as Phil."

Flagg smiled. "That's fine. I understand San Quentin isn't such a bad place, as prisons go."

He shut the door and dropped the heavy wooden crossbar into place. They wouldn't be getting out of there until they were let out. Then he turned to face Lyons again, cowering against the wall."

"What are you going to do to me?" Lyons said. His voice cracked this time, like a woman's.

"Nothing, Ben. Nothing at all."

"What?"

"You're free to go. As soon as I leave, you can walk right on out of here, go where you like, do what you like. But I wouldn't let those other two out, if I were you. They don't like you very much any more; they might just decide to put out your lights for good."

Lyons was shaking his head. "You're going to let me go?"

"Why not? You haven't got anyplace to go, Ben, we

both know that."

The truth finally began to seep in on Lyons. His eyes went wide; Sweat popped out on his face. "No," he said. "No."

Flagg felt no sympathy for him. "You could go to the cops, spill everything in exchange for protection and a new identity. But I wouldn't advise it. That would make the Organization want you dead ten times as badly; and they'd find a way to get to you, no matter how much police protection you had or how good the new identity was. You'd be dead inside a year. And you'd spend that year looking over your shoulder, jumping at every sound, wondering what it was going to happen—"

"Stop it! That's enough!"

Flagg shrugged. He didn't like playing this kind of sadistic role, but it was part of his job, in circumstances such as these, and it had to be done. "What I'd suggest, Ben, is that you start running. Don't even go back to Grants Pass; don't try to draw any money out of the bank or liquidate any of your assets. Just run. And keep on running. You might get away, you never know. You might even find a hole deep enough to crawl in so that nobody ever finds you. At least your odds are a hell of a lot better that way."

He'd said enough; Lyons was close to weeping now. Flagg went over and caught a flaccid arm, steered Lyons to the couch and told him to lie down on it. He did that, bonelessly, and lay with his head buried in his crossed arms.

Flagg went to the gun-cabinet, took all of the weapons and boxes of ammunition out of it and made a quick search of the rest of the cabin. There were no other weapons. He carried the three handguns and two rifles outside, not even looking in Lyons's direction now, and laid them and the ammunition on the front seat of the green pickup.

The keys were in the pickup's ignition. He slid in under the wheel, started the engine and drove to the branch road where he'd left the camper. It had stopped snowing again, but the sky remained threatening. When he saw that the area was still deserted, he backed the pickup to the rear of the camper and managed to transfer the heavy crates to the camper, by means of a two-by-four stretched between the two. Then he swung the pickup around and out of the way, removed the keys and put them under the floor mat. He took the camper back onto the development road, turned toward Fort Rock.

As he drove, he thought that he'd handled things pretty well. The hijacking end of his investigation was more or less closed now. All he had left to do was to stop in Fort Rock, call the Highway Patrol and then call Churlak for instructions on where to drop the leftover crates from the shipment of 'shine equipment; everything after that would be out of his hands and he could concentrate on Burleigh and Ogden and putting the outlaw still out of commission.

He settled back and turned on the AM-FM radio. The AM stations were static-filled and too weak to be heard because of the mountainous terrain; he switched to FM. He went to the end of the dial, started back the other way—and suddenly the cab was filled with a loud, high-pitched squeal. He turned the volume down quickly and stared at the dial: 108.6, where there was no station in the area.

A frigid, clammy feeling seemed to clamp itself between his shoulder-blades. There was only one explanation for the squeal: a homing device had been planted somewhere in the camper and its transmission signal was being picked up by the FM radio.

The homer hadn't been there last night, because he'd tried out the radio on the drive back from Sweetweed; that meant it had to have been installed sometime after he'd gone to bed at the Big Pine, sometime during the early-morning hours. It had been continuously transmitting a piercing FM call to some local receiver ever since he'd left the motel this morning, pinpointing the location of the camper—where it had been, where it was heading. The implications of such a device were what started Flagg sweating.

Who had put it in the camper? Not Lyons, or else he wouldn't have been so surprised at the A-frame. Burleigh? Or somebody else? Who—and *why?*

His foot bore down on the accelerator. The transmitter would not be much good over a fifteen-mile or so radius; whoever was tailing him must be close by—and he had those six crates of bootleg equipment aboard. He had to reach Fort Rock, find the homer and get the hell out of the area before he, they, whoever was back there, realized what was going down.

Beads of sweat laced his forehead and cheeks when he entered the small settlement. He pulled into the first service station he saw off Highway 32, brought the camper to a stop in front of the rest-rooms.

It took him fifteen minutes of feverish searching to

locate the transmitter.

It was tucked behind the right rear fender, attached to the frame by a bar magnet. Flagg ripped it loose, debated dumping it in the trash-barrel outside the rest-rooms and then saw for the first time that there was a supermarket adjacent to the station. The supermarket had a half-filled parking lot and that gave him an idea; instead of leaving the bug here, he would attach it to some housewife's car, leading his followers on a wild-goose chase and giving him a misdirection and the time he needed to get clear of the area.

He vaulted the low brick wall between the station and the supermarket lot and ran to a near group of cars. A woman was just reversing out of a space there. Flagg walked behind her. She braked courteously and he dropped the transmitter on the sheet metal shelf between the body and the bumper of her small Volkswagen beetle.

He pivoted left, walking between two other parked cars to make a circuit back to the camper. As he did, his eyes roamed across the service-station tarmac—and what he saw made him drop reflexively to one knee by the fender of the car on his left.

Two black-and-white Highway Patrol cruisers were pulling onto the tarmac behind the camper.

Flagg clamped his teeth together as the two cruisers jerked to stops and four uniformed officers jumped out with drawn revolvers. They circled the camper, pulling open the cab doors, the rear door. And while they were doing that, another car pulled into the station. It was black, unmarked, and contained two men. The car rocked to a halt and the two men came out running.

Flagg, grimacing, recognized one of them immediately. It was Frank Northrup, the DynaFreight dispatcher. And there was no question that he was the man in charge.

SIXTEEN

Northrup called the Highway Patrolmen together, waving his arms and relaying hurried instructions. It was clear enough to Flagg what they were: search the area, seal it off.

Flagg didn't wait any longer. He eased around the front of the car on his right, still in a low crouch, and ran quickly along the line to the rear of the lot, where it curved around behind the supermarket. When he was out of sight he began to look into the windows of scattered cars, searching for one that had the keys in the ignition.

None of them did.

It was not in Flagg's nature to panic in an emergency. He was sweating again and his chest was tightly constricted, but his thoughts were clear and sharp. He stopped, scanning the surrounding area. Behind the supermarket was a snow-covered slope, not steep but high and exposed; if he tried to go up that way, he would stand out against the white background like a bug on a sheet. A fence bordered the near side of the lot and on the other side he could see another parking lot, a narrower one, that ran behind a line of stores on a street that intersected with Highway 32. A chubby, middle-aged woman with an armload of packages had stopped over there, alongside a dark blue Camaro with snow piled on its roof; she was fumbling in her purse for keys.

Flagg glanced back toward the supermarket. The cops hadn't shown yet, but it wouldn't be long before they did; he had no more than a couple of minutes at the outside. He ran to the fence—a chain-link job, waist-high—and vaulted it sideways, palming the top bar with one hand to lever himself over. The woman at the Camaro had unlocked the passenger door first, deposited the packages inside, and was moving around to the driver's door. Flagg ran in that direction, looking left and right, looking back over his shoulder. There was nobody else in this lot and there were still no uniforms visible near the supermarket.

The woman was already inside the Camaro, shutting the driver's door, when he jerked open the one on the passenger side and slid in beside her, knocking packages to the floor. She made a startled gasping sound, gawking at him. He had no choice; he let her see the .38. That made her squeak like a frightened mouse. Her eyes started to roll up in a faint.

He jabbed her with his free hand, sliding low on the seat so that he couldn't be seen through the rear window. She cringed away from him, but her eyes focused again. And her mouth came open: he could almost hear the shriek that was building in her throat.

Forcing his voice calm, reasonable, he said, "Don't scream, lady. Don't scream and don't panic, and I won't hurt you. You understand? Don't scream and don't panic."

She looked at him, terrified. But her mouth closed and her head wagged up and down.

"All right, good. Now just do what I tell you and I'll be out of your life in twenty minutes. Start the engine, drive out of here, turn right on Highway 32. Do it all slow, normal, just like you're going home with your packages. Can you do that?"

Her head bobbed up and down again. She seemed to have been struck dumb. But she started the car, backed it out of the space, got it pointed into the drive that led to the cross street. She drove rigidly, both hands clamped tight on the wheel, her eyes staring straight ahead—but she didn't do anything to call attention to herself and that was the important thing.

When she stopped at the intersection with Highway 32, he said, "Are there any Highway Patrolmen nearby? I don't mean over at the service station; I mean right around here, looking in this direction."

The first time the woman tried to speak, it came out in a half-strangled gurgle. Then she managed to say the word, "N-no."

"Okay. Make the turn."

She made the turn.

Flagg said, "Take it up to forty-five. Don't drive any faster or any slower."

The woman obeyed. She still wouldn't look at him; she might have had a neck brace on, the way she held her head stiffly in profile to him, looking straight ahead.

Flagg let three minutes of silence go by, watching to make sure she held their speed steady. Then he said, "Anything behind us that looks like a Highway Patrol car?"

"No," she said. The word came out better this time. She was starting to lose some of her terror, to adjust to the situation. She wouldn't be any problem from now on.

Flagg sat up on the seat, turned his head long enough to see that the road behind them was empty, and faced front. They were a few miles outside Lovelock, but he did not want to take the chance of stopping there. Maybe he'd let the woman loose somewhere outside Silverpeak; maybe not. He'd have to see how things looked. As long as she was with him, driving her own car, there was no easy way for the police to pinpoint where he was. But once he let her go and she got to a telephone, they'd know what area he was in and that he was driving a stolen car. Which meant he would have to ditch the car somewhere, out of sight, not long after dumping her.

And then what? Steal another car? Kidnap somebody else? He didn't want to have to do either of those things, not unless he was backed to the wall the way he had been in Fort Rock. The risks were too high; something could go wrong and when things went wrong, somebody usually got hurt. He already had a kidnapping charge against him. He would be as much a fool as Ben Lyons if he willingly put himself in a situation where a murder rap could be added to the list.

Catching a bus was out. He might have to wait too long for one to come along and, even if he could catch one right away, it would close him in, put him in the hands of somebody else with no room to manoeuvre in the event of another emergency. He could call Churlak, of course, get him to send somebody to pick him up with a fresh set of wheels. But that meant explanations, plenty of them, and at least a four-hour wait while Churlak made arrangements and somebody carried them out. Flagg might be able to hole up somewhere that long, but if there was another, faster way to do it, he'd prefer that. He just didn't like having to wait around when things were tight like this.

He let his mind drift back to the homing device in the camper, to Frank Northrup. He knew what had happened as clearly as if he had been watching it on a movie screen. Northrup had been a ringer—a Treasury or FBI agent planted with DynaFreight to listen and observe. That meant that the Feds had somehow gotten wind of the Organization's use of the trucking company to haul illegal goods. The whole DynaFreight operation was blown, and Villareal and Lyons along with it.

Northrup must have suspected Flagg of being just what he was: an undercover Organization troubleshooter. When Lyons had offered to bring him along after the third heist, the one of Flagg's rig, Northrup had readily agreed; and when he'd seen Flagg canvassing the area in a new camper that had magically appeared at the Big Pine, his suspicions had been confirmed. So he had sent for the bug and sometime early this monring he'd attached it to the camper.

And Flagg had led Northrup and his crowd straight to Spruce Hills development, to those twin A-frames. They would have moved in as soon as Flagg left, and probably found Lyons still there, along with the other two, and then decided to close in on Flagg. He'd been damned lucky to get away at all.

It wouldn't mean much if they had Lyons, even with

DynaFreight being blown. Lyons would keep his mouth shut about his knowledge of the Organization because he was a coward and because he'd know it was the only chance he had of staying alive. What did mean something was that the Feds also had the remaining six crates of bootleg equipment.

Had Northrup known about the shipment of mash cookers? Did he know about Burleigh's outlaw still? The answers to both were probably yes. And now that he had evidence of a full-scale moonshining operation in this area, the Feds would be all over the place. The original instructions Flagg and the other troubleshooters had received from Churlak was not only to put the outlaw still out of business, but to salvage as much of the distilling equipment as possible. The salvage end of it didn't look feasible now, with the Feds crawling over the area. But at least he could put the kibosh on Burleigh's operation. Chances were, Northrup and his crowd had no idea where the still was; so it would be up to Flagg, if he could get out of this net he was in, to lead them to that abandoned mine in the Siskiyou wilderness.

Flagg didn't know if that would be enough to satisfy Churlak, coming on top of the DynaFreight mess. But it hadn't been Flagg's fault. How could he have known the camper was bugged? How could he even have *suspected* Northrup was a Fed ringer? Churlak would understand that it wasn't his fault the Feds had got the cases of bootleg equipment and the trucking operation was blown to hell and gone.

He *hoped* Churlak would understand . . .

They were just coming into Lovelock. Flagg glanced

at the chubby woman, but she was still staring straight ahead, still pretending he wasn't there. Her cheeks showed some color now, even though she was still badly frightened. He figured her for a survivalist, just like himself.

Flagg put the .38 under his coat, draped his left arm over the seat back and tried to look like a husband being chauffeured around by his wife as they passed through the village. Nobody paid any attention to them. And there weren't any Highway Patrol cars around that he could see.

When they were through Lovelock, back on open highway again, the woman worked up enough courage to say, "Where are we going?"

"It won't be much longer, lady."

"You're not going to hurt me, are you?"

"I told you I wouldn't and I meant it," Flagg said. "Just relax and enjoy the drive."

She didn't relax, but she no longer seemed quite so tense, either. "All right," she said. "Whatever you say."

Flagg opened up the glove compartment, rummaged through a litter of papers inside and found a road map of the area. He opened it on his lap. He didn't want to go back to Interstate 5, which was liable to be jammed with Highway Patrol units—particularly in the vicinity of the Big Pine Cafe and Motel. He located Lovelock and then found a secondary road that branched off a mile or so outside Silverpeak and wiggled around through a couple of villages until it finally crossed the Oregon border near Mount Ashland. That looked to be his best bet. He refolded the map and put it back inside the glove box.

A mile and a half outside Silverpeak, a Highway Patrol cruiser passed them going the other way. No red light or siren, but it was travelling at a good clip. Flagg looked the other way as the cruiser roared by, pretending to study the scenery.

After another quarter-mile, a picnic area loomed up on the right—just a half-dozen tables scattered in among the trees behind a slush-covered turnaround. Flagg said to the woman, "Pull off on that turnaround up ahead."

She did as she was told. The picnic area, heavily laden with snow, was deserted at this time of year; so was the road in both directions.

"All right," Flagg said. "Get out and go over and sit on one of those benches. Sit there for a half hour; don't move."

"Then what?"

"Then you can do whatever you want. But you'd better wait the full half-hour. Just remember, I'll have this car and I'll know who you are when I look at the registration. If you don't do exactly as I tell you . . ."

She licked dry lips. "Don't worry, I will."

"Good. Okay, get out."

She got out. Flagg waited until she had walked around behind the car, scraped snow off one of the benches and perched herself on it, hugging her purse against her heavy breasts; then he put the Camaro in gear and pulled out onto the highway again.

He had no trouble getting through Silverpeak, even though he saw another Patrol car parked in a service-station lot, watching the highway. There were a pair of tinted glasses in the glove box and Flagg had put them on. He had also covered his head with a fur cap from one of the packages that had popped open when he'd knocked it to the floor back in Fort Rock.

He also had no trouble finding the turnoff for the secondary road, and none after he was on it. He drove some fifteen miles and passed through two hamlets so small they were nothing more than a few buildings crowded alongside the road. The sky remained overcast, but there were no snow flurries. By the time he neared the first sizable community in the area, Brooknoll, he had an idea of what he was going to do. He wasn't happy with it, but it was the fastest way for him to get clear.

There were scattered houses on the near outskirts of Brooknoll, so he went through the little town looking for an isolated area and a side road. He found both less than a half-mile distant: a section of dense forestland, heavy with ferns and underbrush, and a narrow country lane slanting off through it. He turned onto the lane, found a place where he could pull the Camaro off into a snow-bank and wedged it there between a couple of pines. Its tail end could be seen from the lane, he discovered half a minute later; he packed snow over the license plate. But it didn't really matter. It would be a while before anybody stumbled on the car in here.

Still wearing the fur cap, he walked back down the road and into Brooknoll. Three cars passed him on the way, tires spraying slush, but none of them was the law. On one of the side streets in the village was a cafe that had a telephone booth in the rear. Flagg changed two dollar bills into extra silver and then shut himself up inside the booth.

The first thing he did was to call Information for the Medford area and ask for a listing on Toni Kenyon. He half-expected that she wouldn't have a phone, but he was wrong. And his luck continued to hold; when he dialled the number the Information operator gave him, Toni's voice answered on the fourth ring.

"This is Jim Harter," he said.

"Jim! Well, this is a surprise."

"I was hoping you'd be in."

"You just caught me. This is my night off and I was going out to dinner and a movie."

"Alone?"

"Yes. Why?"

"Toni, look, I need your help. Have you got a car?"

"Sure I've got a car. What is it, Jim?"

"I'm stuck in a little town on the California side of the border, called Brooknoll. Do you know where that is?"

"No, but I can find it on a map. Are you in some kind of trouble? You sound . . . urgent."

"It's not big trouble," he lied, "but it is urgent. Will you come?"

"Of course I will."

"Good. It shouldn't take you more than a couple of hours."

"I'll be there as fast as I can."

"You're a lifesaver." Literally, he thought. "I'm in a place called the Brooknoll Cafe, on Klamath Street just off the main drag. I'll wait for you here."

He pronged the receiver, debated calling Churlak and decided to wait. He went out and found a place to sit at the counter. The clock on the wall above the grill said that it was almost five. He wasn't hungry, but he ordered a cheeseburger and a cup of coffee. Eating would help him pass the time.

Then he sat and watched the clock, watched the street outside. And waited.

SEVENTEEN

It was ten past seven when Toni arrived. Flagg was working on his eighth cup of coffee, smoking his pipe and passing the time with one of the waitresses. He had needed an excuse for sitting in there so long, to keep any of the employees from becoming suspicious, so he had struck up a conversation with the waitress and told her he was waiting for his wife to finish shopping.

As soon as he saw Toni come in, he said, "There she is—finally," and swung off his stool. He laid a five-dollar bill on the counter, told the waitress to keep the change. He caught Toni's arm before she could say anything and steered her back outside.

"Where's your car?" he asked her.

"Just up the street. Jim, are you all right?"

"Fine, now."

She kept looking at him, biting her lip, as they made their way along the deserted sidewalk. Her expression showed concern. She had changed her attitude toward him, all right. The reason didn't matter, not right now; but it still occurred to him to wonder why.

Her car was a battered old Edsel, of all things. When she got her keys out of her purse, Flagg said, "Do you mind if I do the driving?"

"No, I guess not."

She gave him the keys, went around to the passenger side. Flagg slid in under the wheel. Half a minute later, he had them on the road heading north out of Brooknoll.

Toni kept watching him, toying with a lock of her taffy blonde hair. After a time, she said, "Where are we going?"

"Back up your way."

"Sweetweed?"

"No. A place called Applegate, on Highway 238."

"Why there?"

"I've got business in that area."

"You mean that abandoned mine I told you about?"

"That's what I mean."

"You're not going up there tonight, in the dark?"

"No. First thing tomorrow. I'll get a motel for the night. There are some things I have to take care of before I go check out the mine."

"What things?"

"Some calls I have to make," Flagg said, "business calls. I can't tell you any more than that."

"Can you tell me why you were stuck in that little town, without any car?"

"No. I'm sorry, Toni."

"Sure. I understand."

They rode in silence for five or six miles. Flagg did not see any sign of the law, which meant that the chubby woman's Camaro hadn't been found yet. He wondered again, as he had in the Brooknoll Cafe, how extensive the manhunt for him was. And decided again that it couldn't be too extensive or he'd have seen more cops around during the past few hours, maybe even run into a roadblock or two coming over from Fort Rock or heading up into Oregon as they were doing now. They were looking for him, no question about that; but they had turned DynaFreight, they had Lyons and the hijackers, they probably also had Villareal by this time, and an Organization troubleshooter was small potatoes compared to all of that.

Besides which, Northrup and the state cops wouldn't know his real name—not unless Lyons or Villareal spilled it, and that wasn't likely. Northrup knew him only as Eric Scofield. He'd have broadcast Flagg's description, and the Scofield alias, but with any luck, that would be all they had to go on. Even if they found latent fingerprints in the room he'd occupied at the Big Pine, it wouldn't do them any good: Flagg had never been in the armed forces and had never been arrested, much less convicted of anything, so his prints weren't on record anywhere.

Toni wanted to put the radio on, but he said he didn't want the distraction. The truth was, he didn't want her to pick up any news bulletins that might be broadcast. She hadn't heard any on the way down or she'd have been sure to make the connection that he was the man the Highway Patrol and the Feds were after.

To keep her mind off the radio, he decided to make conversation. He asked her, "Anything new at the tavern?"

"Not that I could tell. I went in for a little while this afternoon, but that's all. It's my day off, like I said on the phone."

"Was Ogden there?"

"No. The bartender said he went somewhere for the day."

"He have any idea where?"

"No."

"Any sign of Burleigh?"

"Not while I was around."

They talked about other things after that, one of which was Toni herself. He got her to open up a little about her background: She was twenty-nine, had been working at the New Old Lompoc House for a little over a year, ever since her second husband had divorced her so he could marry a nineteen-year-old topless dancer in Portland. He'd been a truck driver, she said. Her first husband had been an auto supply salesman, and why she kept getting mixed up with jerks who had automotive careers, she didn't know. Maybe she just had a talent for picking losers. She said that matter-of-factly, but there was a tinge of bitterness in her voice. The job at the New Old Lompoc House paid good wages and the tips were big on the weekends; that was why she'd plunked herself down in a place like Sweetweed. But she wasn't planning on staying there much longer — another six months at the outside. That is, if Morley Ogden wasn't arrested for his bootlegging activities and the New Old Lompoc House shut down for good. Either way, when she left she'd probably go up to Portland again and see what she could find there.

She meant in the way of a job, but she'd probably find herself another husband too. Flagg had known women like her before—good women who had a knack for picking bad men, who kept drifting around trying to put their lives on some sort of meaningful keel—and they seemed to prefer being married. Most of the time they kept picking losers, one right after another. He hoped that when Toni decided on Number Three, the guy was somebody who deserved her.

When they crossed the border into Oregon, Flagg told Toni to get out her road map and direct them to Highway 238. She said she didn't need the map, she knew how to get them there. And she did, without any trouble. Less than an hour later, using mostly secondary roads, they picked up Highway 238 and drove on into Applegate.

Flagg stopped at the first motel he saw with a Vacancy sign. He signed in, got a room for himself and drove the car in and parked it in front. Then he turned to look at Toni.

"End of the line," he said. "Now I go do some work."

"And I go back to Sweetweed?"

"Isn't that what you want to do?"

"Not particularly," she said. She tugged at the lock of hair again, as she had during most of the drive. "I wish I knew more about you, Jim."

"No you don't," Flagg said. "I'm not a good person to know a lot about."

"I think you are." She looked at him for a moment. "I don't have to leave right away," she said. "I could go and buy us a pizza or something while you make your phone calls. Or do you just want me to leave?"

Flagg debated. Maybe it wouldn't be a bad idea if she stayed around for a while. It would keep her from listening to the radio or watching television and finding out he wasn't a Federal agent after all. He didn't think she would give him away even if she did find out, but this way he could keep an eye on her for a while longer.

"No, don't leave yet," he said. "Give me a half-hour of privacy. I should be finished with the calls by then."

She nodded, smiling. "What kind of pizza do you like?"

"Anything you like."

"I'll buy some beer too," she said.

He got out and let her have the wheel. Then he opened up his room and when he had the door locked behind him he sat on the double bed, picked up the telephone. Churlak's voice was yelling in his ear a few seconds later.

"Where the hell have you been? Christ, I thought the Feds must've busted you too."

"So you know what's been going down?"

"Yeah, I know what's been going down. Flagg, what's the matter with you? You never screwed up like this before."

"It wasn't my fault," Flagg said. He went on to explain things the way he'd figured them—the bug in the camper, Northrup being a Federal plant, the way he'd handled Lyons and the two hijackers. He finished with, "There wasn't anything I could do to hold DynaFreight together. The Feds must have had it spotted for months; it was only a matter of time before they moved in."

"Maybe so, but you still let them get those crates of 'shine equipment."

"Yeah, I know. Maybe I should have swept the camper. But who'd figure it for a bug? Hell, it was clean yesterday."

"All right, all right," Churlak said. "I'm just blowing off steam. We're not holding you responsible —at least not to the point where you get slapped on the wrist."

Flagg knew what that meant. He didn't say anything.

"What a lousy mess," Churlak said. "Now we've got to start all over again up in that territory, open a new freight line somewhee. That'll take months and a hell of a lot of money."

"Did the Feds raid DynaFreight?"

"You bet your ass they raided DynaFreight. Records, some stored goods, a dozen trucks—they got everything. It'll cost us a million or more."

"Villareal?"

"Villareal, too. But he won't tell them anything."

"What about Lyons? They get him?"

"Sure they got him, the bastard. We figured he had to be the Judas from the way he was busted."

"He won't talk," Flagg said. "He's a coward and I think I handled him right."

"He won't if he knows what's good for him. So where've you been since you abandoned the camper? Last report I had, you'd kidnapped some woman and swiped her car."

Flagg told him the rest of it.

"Why the hell didn't you call earlier?"

"I wanted to clear out of California first, light someplace safe," Flagg said. "And it was easier using the woman to help me—faster."

"You back in Oregon now?"

"Yeah. A place called Applegate on Highway

238—the Restful View Motel, room twelve. Under the Jim Harter name."

"Restful View. Shit. You sure you can trust this woman?"

"Sure enough. She thinks I'm a Federal agent myself."

"Terrific," Churlak said sourly. "All right, what about the outlaw still? Have you got anything more on that?"

"Plenty. I told you yesterday I thought I knew where it is; now I'm ninety percent sure. As soon as I make it positive, I can shut Burleigh down quick and easy."

"How?"

"Sic the Feds on the still."

"That doesn't get our cookers back for us. Or any of their equipment to help recoup our losses."

"I know it, "Flagg said. "But the area is crawling with FBI and ATF agents as it is. If we try to stage a raid, it's liable to backfire; and a big shootout would only get the governmnet even hotter than they already are. Burleigh's got that still heavily guarded. No matter who goes in there, there's bound to be gunplay. Why not let the Feds get shot up?"

"Makes sense," Churlak agreed grudgingly. "I hate to lose all that equipment, but it doesn't look like we've got much choice. All right, then——handle it your way."

"I'll need a new set of wheels. And before dawn."

"Why before dawn?"

"I want to go in early, while everything is quiet and sleepy. Sooner I report to you and you let the Feds hear about it, the better."

"Can you get in there? I thought you said the place

was heavily guarded."

"It is, but there's an auxiliary mine entrance on the opposite side of the hill. A kind of back door. I think I can get in and out that way."

"Anything else you need?"

"Another handgun. Make it a .38 with a silencer. And a couple of grenades, just in case. Hiking boots, a backpack, some hiking clothes—Levi's, a Pendleton shirt, some kind of cap. That should do it. I could also use a toilet kit," he added as an afterthought. "All my gear got left at the Big Pine."

"It'll all be there by four a.m." Churlak paused. "Two things, Flagg."

Flagg knew what was coming. He waited.

"Don't get yourself killed, poking around that still. You're still the best troubleshooter we've got."

"I plan on staying alive," Flagg said.

"The second thing is this: Don't screw up again."

And Churlak banged the receiver down in his ear.

Flagg grimaced, dropped his own handset into its cradle. Then he went into the bathroom, washed his face, dried off. He was checking the load in his .38 Special when the knock sounded on the door. He went over there, holding the gun in his right hand, but it was only Toni. He put the .38 in its holster, the holster inside one of the nightstand drawers, and then opened up for her.

She had a pizza carton and a six-pack of beer. "I got a pepperoni," she said. "I hope that's okay."

"Fine."

"Are you finished with your calls?"

"All finished," Flagg said.

They ate at the small table the room provided. Flagg had two beers with the pizza and felt himself beginning to unwind a little. Toni seemed to be in an expansive mood, chattering on, touching his hand every now and then. He thought that she was a damned good-looking woman when she was wearing regular clothes—a grey wool dress tonight—instead of that 1928 Tart's costume Ogden had her parading around in at the New Old Lompoc House.

When they were done eating, Toni went in to use the bathroom. Flagg looked at his watch. Almost eleven. He'd have to get to bed pretty quick if he was going to catch any sleep before Churlak's newest courier showed up.

Toni came out and he saw that she'd combed her hair. And when she came over near him, he could smell the musky fragrance of the perfume she'd daubed herself with. She said, "It's getting late. I can go now if you want."

He didn't say anything, watching her.

"Or I can stay if you want," she said.

Flagg still didn't say anything. He was thinking it over.

She came forward a couple of steps, close. "Do you want me to stay, Jim? I will if you want me to."

He made up his mind. He wasn't *that* tired, and she really was a good-looking woman, and being with her would help him unwind even more. He nodded and said, "I want you to."

Another step; now their bodies were touching. Toni's mouth parted and her arms came up around his neck. The kiss was long, intense. When she broke it she stepped back a pace, moistening her lips. And then reached behind her for the zipper on her dress.

She was naked underneath it.

A long time later they both slept, Flagg lightly, the way he always did when he was working under pressure. His internal alarm-clock woke him up a few minutes past three. Churlak's courier hadn't shown up yet, but Churlak had promised he'd be there by four and he would be.

Gently, Flagg woke Toni up. "You're not going to like me for this," he said, "but I've got to ask you to leave."

"What time is it?"

"After three."

She sat up blinking when he switched on the nightstand lamp. "What's the matter, Jim?"

"Somebody'll be coming by pretty soon and I'd better be alone. Then I've got things to do, preparations to make."

"All right," she said reluctantly. "Whatever you say, Jim."

She got out of bed, made a brief trip into the bathroom, came out and dressed. Flagg was dressed, too, by that time, packing tobacco into his pipe. She came over to him and held his face between her hands, looking into his eyes.

"You could get to be a habit, you know that?" she said.

"Don't make me one. You'll only get hurt."

"Oh, I didn't mean it like that. You don't let people get involved with you, I can tell that. It's your job, isn't it?"

"Yes."

"Well, don't worry, I understand. I knew how it would be all along, but the more I saw of you, the more it didn't seem to matter. We had tonight, and tonight was very good, wasn't it?"

"The best," he said, meaning it.

"Will I see you again? At least once more?"

"If it's possible, you will." He meant that, too.

She kissed him. "You know where to find me," she said, and moments later she was gone.

Flagg sat in one of the chairs, smoking his pipe, waiting. At five minutes to four, Churlak's courier showed up with a 1978 Ford Falcon pickup, told him everything he'd asked for was stored behind the seat, and left with somebody in a trailing car. Flagg took the gear from behind the seat, carried it inside. He dressed in the Levi's and Pendleton and hiking boots, slid into his corduroy jacket. His .38 Special went into one jacket pocket; he put the silenced .38 into a specially built scabbard that had been provided with the Levi's and was attached to a pair of the belt loops. He stowed the two fragmentation grenades inside the backpack, carried the backpack out to the Falcon.

At 4:45 he was on his way into the Siskiyou wilderness.

EIGHTEEN

He found the old logging road Toni had told him about without difficulty. When he passed the private mine road—there were no guards out this early, or at least none that he could see—he began checking the Falcon's odometer. After four and three-quarters miles, the rain-swollen creek looped down to parallel the highway; and after five and two-tenths miles, he saw the remains of the bridge looming up in the first grey light of dawn.

A little ways farther on was a turnaround. Flagg pulled in there, parked the Falcon. Strapping on the backpack, he made his way along the side of the road until he found a place where he could ford the stream. No cars passed him; the area looked and felt deserted.

The logging road began just beyond the rotting bridge timbers. It was as overgrown as Toni had led him to believe: high grass, berry bushes, encroaching tangles of underbrush and ferns. At first he had a little trouble following the mostly obliterated track, but as it began to wind upward through spruce and redwood trees, the undergrowth thinned out some and he was able to discern the road's course more easily.

As he went, he reviewed what Toni had told him about the abandoned mine, the auxiliary tunnel. Logic told him that the Tru-test tankers would drive through the gravel-pit and inside the main shaft of the mine, where the cookers had to be, and load from the vats in there. The auxiliary tunnel would probably connect with the main shaft, the way such tunnels almost always did. It figured that there would be other passages inside the mountain as well; that would explain the still's ventilation system, why Flagg and the other Organization troubleshooters had seen nothing when they grid-checked by air. And an underground stream, maybe one that fed the creek down below, would no doubt supply the water and carry off the waste, which would be well-filtered by the time it reached ground level.

If he was right about all of this, it would make the Feds' job easy for them. They could come up the way he was coming, get in through the auxiliary tunnel, seal off the passages and take Burleigh's men inside the main shaft. Or chase them back down the private road into the arms of another wave of agents. But Flagg still had to make sure. If he was wrong about the lay of things, but went ahead and notified the Feds anyway, and they went in and got themselves cut to pieces, the stink that would cause would make things twice as hot for the Organization. When Churlak gave him a job to do he didn't want half measures or anything that could lead to a backlash. That was particularly true now, after the DynaFreight fiasco.

Churlak's last words to him still echoed inside Flagg's head: *Don't screw up again.*

He kept slogging upward along what was left of the logging road, trying to look like a solitary hiker. But his eyes and ears keened his surroundings at every step. Twenty minutes passed, and still the half-obliterated track continued its winding ascent. Flagg couldn't see any sign of the mine yet, not through the closely knit canopy of tree branches overhead and above.

The main things he had to worry about, he kept reminding himself, were guards and sensor devices. Maybe dogs, too. But Burleigh's crowd couldn't afford to have the area *too* well-guarded. There were bound to be picnickers and hikers in this wilderness during the spring and summer months, and they'd become suspicious if they encountered a buildup of men and warning systems. On the other hand, Burleigh had to know by now that there were Federal agents in the vicinity, that they'd turned DynaFreight and grabbed Lyons. If he was afraid Lyons would tell the Feds about the still, and about their hijacking arrangement, he might already have beat it out of the state. Yet he'd have no reason to close down the still itself, since Lyons didn't know where it was, and hadn't told Burleigh who Flagg was. What Burleigh would do, whether he cut and ran or not, was to order increased security around the mine, in an effort to keep the area from being breached.

Up ahead, the road jogged in a sharp dogleg to the left. Flagg started into the curve, moving silently and staying in the protective cover of a high growth of juniper. He was halfway through when he spotted the first guard, on the far side of the thicket—a heavy-set man in an old plaid jacket and a deer-hunter's cap, armed with a rifle. The man was sitting on a high, flat-topped rock, half-turned away from the road where it bent in his direction; from that position, he could look up the track and down it into the curve. He hadn't reckoned on anyone seeing him through the screen of juniper or he would have concealed himself better.

Flagg stood still, watching the guard for a time. The man kept tossing pebbles at a rotted log ten yards away from him; he looked bored and cold. Every now and then he took a swallow from a thermos jug of coffee, maybe laced with something stronger to chase away the chill.

Slowly and carefully, Flagg backed down the road until he was out of the dogleg. Then he veered off to his left, making his way through the trees, climbing upward in a rough parallel to the road. The trees and undergrowth screened him from the juniper thicket; he could just see patches of it through vegetation, a glimpse now and then of the guard. The man didn't move from the flat-topped rock.

Flagg stayed in the trees until he was well above where the guard sat and the road had jogged away to the east. When he was certain he couldn't be seen from below, he cut over to the track again and continued the climb along its rutted, muddy surface.

It was another ten minutes before he saw the mine tower—a crumbling wooden structure outlined against the overcast sky in gloomy emphasis. The road curved again ahead of him and when he came through the curve, still silent and still keeping to cover, he saw the narrow rusted line of ore-cart tracks Toni had mentioned. They came down a long grassy slope and ended in what had once been some kind of platform; now, there was nothing to mark the spot except a jumble of decomposing timbers. The slope was flanked by jagged outcroppings and dense vegetation that made easy passage around to the far side of the hill, where the main mine entrance was, an impossibility. From where he stood, the entrance to the auxiliary tunnel, seventy or eighty yards above, was hidden by a pair of large boulders.

He started up through the damp grass. Three-quarters of the way along, he heard what sounded like a low growling from behind the nearest of the boulders. His stomach muscles tensed. And in the next instant a man came out into view, cradling a rifle in the crook of one arm; the other hand held the leash of a lean, savage-looking Doberman.

The man said sharply, "Just hold it right there, buddy." As if to add a menacing agreement of its own, the dog made another low growling sound; its yellowish eyes were narrowed beads of hate.

Flagg stopped. There was only one way to play this now, and he knew it and accepted it. He made himself look surprised and puzzled. He said, "Who're you?"

"Never mind that. What're you doing up here?"

"Hiking," Flagg said. "I'm a hiker. What's going on?"

"This is private property. No trespassing."

"No kidding? I didn't know that."

"Well, now you do."

"Whose property is it?"

"Northwest Mining Association," the man said. "You're not going to give me any hassle, are you?"

"Not me. No hassle at all."

Flagg pivoted to his left, making it look casual, his right arm sliding across the front of his body. The silenced .38 came out of its scabbard smoothly. He turned all the way around, not hurrying it, and faced uphill again. He shot the guard first, because the rifle was leveled toward him. The man made a surprised noise, dropped the rifle, let go of the leash and fell over on his face, skidding downward past Flagg at an angle. The Doberman launched itself in a snarling attack. Flagg had just enough time to sidestep and shoot the animal in mid-air; it sailed past him, landed in-between the ore tracks and rolled all the way down to the bottom of the slope.

There was a little noise, most of it from the tumbling bodies; but if there were any other guards in the vicinity, they might take it for a rockslide. Flagg went down and checked the guard. Dead, all right: the .38's bullet had drilled a hole through his heart. Then he hurried the rest of the way upslope, took a position behind the boulder where he could look down toward the logging road. It must have been the same position the guard had been in earlier; Flagg had an unobstructed view of the road and the surrounding trees.

He waited ten minutes, playing it safe. When nobody else showed up in that time, he turned toward the tunnel entrance.

The timbers of the tower were riddled with termites and worms and dry-rot and the structure looked near collapse. The iron elevator wheel tilted where a support had fallen away. Debris cluttered the rocky ground. Off on one side was a crude stone fireplace and chimney, all that remained of a small mine office. The mouth of the tunnel itself was shored up with more rotting timbers, and more debris and a long mound of earth and rock like a decayed tongue spilled out of the blackness within.

Flagg eased his way inside, taking out his pen-flash. He shielded the light with his handkerchief and switched it on. In its faint light he could see that part of the tunnel had caved in, with piles of earth and shale and fallen beams choking the passage. What was left of the tunnel's ceiling was a foot over his head. Dust and the smell of decay clogged his nostrils as he moved forward in slow, cautious steps.

Five minutes passed. A collapsed section of the tunnel forced him to abandon the backpack and crawl part of the way on his hands and knees. But he took the time to transfer the two fragmention grenades into his jacket pocket before he unstrapped the pack. He couldn't afford to leave any of his firepower behind, not closed in the way he was now.

As soon as he was able to stand again, he reached a dead end; the tunnel was completely blocked. At first he thought it was the result of another, heavier cave-in, but then he realized that the obstruction had been man-made. This must be where the tunnel gave access into the main shaft.

He played the flash along the wall of dirt and rock. Near the top, he found a small opening which looked as though it might pass through to the other side. He dug at the space, enlarging it, working as silently as he was able. Inside of ten minutes he had dug a burrow wide enough for him to squeeze partway into. And when he did that he was staring down a long incline at a widened grotto in the mine's main shaft.

The still was there.

The boiler and distillation column jutted upward, disappearing into the rock, probably to another tunnel. Steam rose faintly in the murky, floodlit cavern. He could see five large vats clustered at one end, with piping to carry the mash to the column. Even as near as he was, he could not smell much of the fermentation process; the vats were well-covered. Two men worked at a control panel full of gauges and valves; two more stood guard at the yawning entrance at the far end—an entrance more than wide enough to accommodate one of the Tru-test tankers, with parking space inside for at least two. Flagg felt a small grudging admiration for the still's architect. It may have been turning out an inferior product, but whoever had designed it was a thorough professional.

He lay peering into the grotto for another five minutes, studying the layout, fixing the location of everything in his mind so he could relay it accurately to Churlak. Then, satified, he got ready to ease himself backward out of the burrow.

But he didn't do it. In that moment the sound of a car engine echoed through the mine, and a sleek black car appeared at the entrance and slid inside. Flagg recognized it as Vincent Burleigh's Lincoln Continental.

The car stopped at an angle near the vats. Three people got out of it, into the murky light; Flagg could see them well enough to recognize them too. His body tensed again, his teeth clamped together in a tight-jawed grimace. Under his breath he said, "Damn."

One of those who got out of the Continental was

Burleigh. Morley Ogden was the second man. The third person was a woman.
  Toni Kenyon.

NINETEEN

Flagg squinted into the semi-gloom, trying to gauge the situation. Ogden had hold of Toni's arm and was steering her to where a wooden table and several folding chairs were arranged between the vats and the control panel. He shoved her roughly into one of the chairs. She glared up at him, said something that Flagg couldn't hear up where he was. But it must have enraged Ogden; he slapped her across the face, with such vicious force that it almost sent her toppling out of the chair.

Ogden looked as if he wanted to hit her again, but Burleigh called something to him and Ogden backed off to join him. The two of them held some sort of conference with the men at the control panel. Toni sat stiffly in the chair, not touching her cheek where Ogden had slapped her, looking around at the grotto and the components of the still with what seemed to be wonder.

She wasn't mixed up with Burleigh and Ogden, wasn't part of the outlaw operation. That was what Flagg had thought when he'd first seen her—that she'd lied to him all along, played him for a sucker. But the way Ogden had manhandled her, the way she kept looking around at things, told him it couldn't be that way. So did the fact that she had known for days that he was onto Burleigh, and also known he was coming out here today; if she was one of the opposition, she'd have told Burleigh about him and his plans and a dozen men would have been laying for him when he showed up this morning.

All right, but then why the hell had they brought her here? Why the rough stuff? The only thing Flagg could figure was that she'd decided to poke her nose into things at the New Old Lompoc House, for whatever crazy reason of her own, and Ogden had caught her at it. That didn't explain why he and Burleigh had decided to bring her out here, but that was something he could find out later on.

The big question now was, what was he going to do about her?

Training and instinct told him he shouldn't do anything about her. Just leave her here, get out himself, call Churlak and let the Feds come riding to the rescue. That was the smart thing to do. But it was also coldblooded, maybe too coldblooded for him. It would take at least a day, perhaps two, for the ATF and FBI boys to mobilize an attack force against the still; Burleigh and Ogden could be long gone by then, and Toni could be long dead. They wouldn't take her along with them if they ran for it; there was no percentage in that. And they wouldn't turn her loose to testify against them. If they'd brought her here, were letting her see where the still was located, it had to mean they were planning to kill her sooner or later.

Christ, Flagg thought, he couldn't leave her to be

murdered. It was one thing to kill somebody like that guard outside, an enemy, a hardcase who played the same survival-of-the-fittest game that Flagg played; it was another thing to kill somebody like Toni, an innocent, a woman he'd slept with and loved a little less than twelve hours ago. And he *would* be killing her if he went off and left her to the mercy of Burleigh and Ogden, just as sure as if he pulled the trigger himself. Do that, and he'd hate himself for the rest of his life.

That was the trouble with him, that was why he wasn't really a good Organization man and would never move up into its hierarchy: He had a soft core, despite the outer plates of armour. He had a conscience.

Burleigh and Ogden kept on conferring with the two still workers. Toni was staring at them now, her arms wrapped across her chest as if she were cold; she wore the same outfit—tight corduroy pants and a ski jacket —that she had the night she'd surprised him inside the New Old Lompoc House. Flagg gave his attention to the incline that stretched downward from where he was to the grotto. Rusted ore-cart tracks led along it and off to the left, behind where the cookers were. Mounds of earth, stacks of timber, piles of rock littered both sides of the tracks—leftovers and castaways from the construction of the still. They offered some cover, maybe just enough. The main problem, Flagg thought, was getting out of this burrow without making noise and down the slope without slipping or starting a small slide. The incline wasn't steep and the footing looked to be mostly solid rock. If he could get down to the vats, he could work his way around to where Toni was at the table . . .

He lay there watching, waiting to see what Burleigh and Ogden and the other two would do. The conference lasted another couple of minutes; then Burleigh got back into his Continental, alone, and drove out through the mine entrance. Ogden and one of the other men went outside on foot—cigarette break or catch some fresh air. The second man had been assigned to watch Toni; he crossed to the table and sat down in a chair facing her. That left him and the two armed guards at the entrance, neither of whom was looking anywhere inside the grotto.

Now or never, Flagg thought.

He wiggled forward, easing himself through the hole. He had a good six feet of tunnel in front of him before the incline began; what little dirt and pebbles sifted out from his passage fell on the horizontal floor, rather than tumbled down the slope. The pebbles made small sounds against the rock, but with the bubbling of the steam cookers, they couldn't be heard below.

Flagg crawled to the edge of the incline, drew the silenced .38, made sure none of the three men was looking in his direction and then started down. He moved in a crouch, watching where he put his feet, weaving sideways among the mounds of earth and rock and lumber. He stopped and went to one knee each time any of the men below stirred. But none of them even glanced up at the incline. And neither Ogden nor the other distiller returned from outside.

It took him a full five minutes to reach the shadows behind the vat nearest the slope. Down close like this, he could smell the heavy yeasty odour of the 'shine; he started to breathe through his mouth. He worked his way from vat to vat, along the wall side. When he got to the space between the first and second, he edged in-between them and peered around at the table where Toni and her guard were sitting.

Toni was facing in his direction, the distiller half-facing toward the entrance. She didn't see Flagg yet, but she would as soon as he made his move. Beyond her, the two men at the entrance had drifted together and were talking. One of them lit a cigarette. Flagg still couldn't see Ogden or the other distiller, though most of the area directly in front of the mine was visible from where he was standing.

Flagg thumbed the hammer back on the silenced .38, stepped out of the shadows between the vats.

When Toni saw him, her eyes went wide and he could hear the sudden sharp intake of her breath. She half-rose out of her chair. The distiller swiveled head and body, started to get up too, but Flagg, moving ever since he'd exposed himself, got to the man before he could do anything or make any kind of noise, and clouted him above the ear with the .38's long barrel tube. The impact was solid enough to shatter bone; the man grunted, pitched sideways toward the table. Flagg caught him before he banged into it, using his free left arm, and lowered the limp figure across the tabletop.

The rest of it might have gone just as smoothly and quietly, and he might have got Toni and himself out of there with a minimum of hassle, if she hadn't managed to kick over her chair in her excitement.

It happened when she started toward him, wearing a look of amazement and relief. Her foot caught one leg of the chair, kicked it up and sent the thing clattering to the rock floor. The noise the falling chair made in that hollowed-out mine was like a gunshot; echoes rolled and bounced off the stone walls. The two guards at the entrance whirled away from each other, peering toward the vats. Flagg had caught hold of Toni's wrist and was already dragging her between the first two cookers; but it was obvious they'd been seen. No sooner were they into the shadows than the first shot cracked out, the first bullet made a whining ricochet off the rock at Flagg's heels.

Toni may have been terrified, but she had courage; she didn't cling all over him and she didn't panic when he let go of her wrist. "Do exactly what I tell you," he snapped at her. "Stay behind me, keep your head down."

They were almost to the incline now, running from the fourth vat to the fifth. Ahead, on the slope, was one of the stacks of lumber. Flagg looked back over his shoulder to see where the pursuit was. And one of the guards was just emerging from between the first two vats.

"Behind the lumber!" Flagg yelled at Toni. Without waiting to see if she obeyed, he swung around in a crouch and fired twice at the guard. Both shots missed, but the bullets went by close enough to drive the man back into the shadows.

Flagg was moving again the instant after he triggered the .38, running for the stack of lumber. He didn't see Toni until after he threw himself, sliding, around behind the stack; she crouched there, unhurt, eyes as big as saucers. Two seconds after he gained the cover, another rifle shot sent more ringing echoes through the grotto.

Flagg moved around Toni, gesturing for her to follow him. He went along the stack to its end. From there he could see past the cookers, past the control panel and the maze of overhead piping to where the boiler was. Ogden and the second distiller had been alerted by the shooting and were back inside the mine; the tavern owner was just scurrying out of sight behind the boiler. Four men, Flagg thought, four against one and an unarmed woman. Four guns, maybe more, and at least two of them semi-automatic rifles. He didn't like those odds worth a damn, not with fifty yards of slope to cross in an upward trajectory to where the auxiliary tunnel was, and a narrow hole to crawl through besides.

But he had something to equalize the odds, maybe turn them in his and Toni's favor. A couple of somethings. He would have preferred not to use them, but he had no choice now.

He took out one of the fragmentation grenades.

Toni's eyes got even bigger when she saw the ugly little grey pineapples, but she didn't say anything. Flagg pointed upslope, showing her the route they would travel, indicating where the cover was and where the ore-cart tracks led into the auxiliary tunnel. She nodded, letting him know she understood.

Flagg looked over the lumber again. He couldn't see any of the four men—not that it mattered too much where they were deployed. If he could put the grenade where he wanted it, over near those cookers, the explosion would keep them too busy to do any more shooting.

He pulled the pin, held the lever tightly depressed against his palm while he gauged distance and angle. Then he straightened up long enough to toss the grenade in an overhand arc. He didn't wait to see where it hit; he pulled Toni over against him, shoved her head down and wedged both of them back against the lumber.

One of the men out there shouted—a cry of terror. He was still yelling when the grenade blew.

The explosion was thunderous in that big stone room and it was followed almost immediately by a second, even more booming blast as one of the cookers erupted. Mash and 'shine and steam burst upward, filled the grotto and unleashed an overpowering alcohol smell; the concussion shook the ground, the walls, sent little avalanches of rock and dirt sliding down the incline from above. The echoes went on and on. Underneath them, Flagg could hear somebody screaming, pieces of shrapnel clattering off stone.

As soon as the echoes began to die, he pulled Toni to her feet and ran with her upslope, dodging behind cover near the cart tracks, trying to keep his footing on the dislodged carpeting of pebbles and earth. Nobody shot at them. Nobody was likely to do any more shooting in there; the clouds of steam from the burst cooker reduced visibility to zero and it would have been like trying to shoot through a fogbank.

Whoever it was that was screaming kept right on doing it until Flagg and Toni reached the auxiliary tunnel; then it cut off like a dying siren. The hole Flagg had scraped out earlier was partially filled in again from the explosions. He went to all fours, began digging into earth and rock, and Toni knelt to help him. It took them two minutes to clear the space wide enough so that she could squeeze through.

While she was doing that, Flagg took the second grenade out of his jacket and jerked the pin. The steam was just starting to dissipate when he hurled the pineapple at the boiler. He heard it bounce, thud against something. And he was on his knees, just starting to crawl into the hole after Toni, when it blew.

Earth and pieces of rock sifted down on his back from the new concussion, but none of it did any damage to him. He wiggled all the way through, got to his feet, switched on his penlight. Toni caught onto his arm. She looked shaky, but it was tension more than fear; she wasn't going to fall apart on him.

The boiler exploded just after they crawled past the partial obstruction of the tunnel he'd encountered earlier. The eruption seemed twice as thunderous as the previous two. The tunnel walls trembled; Flagg heard rocks falling, was bathed in sudden showers of dirt. The whole damn shaft was liable to cave in at any minute.

He ran forward as fast as he dared with the uncertain footing; Toni was close behind him, still hanging onto his arm. Down in the main shaft, there were more explosions as the rest of the cookers went up. When the daylit tunnel mouth appeared ahead of them, Toni made a little whimpering moan of relief. But Flagg slowed as they neared it, watchful for any sign of the one guard he'd seen and bypassed earlier. The debris-ridden area outside the tunnel appeared empty. He pulled Toni in close to one wall, told her to stay there and went out first to fan the area with his .38.

There was nobody around.

Some of the urgency drained out of him. He motioned Toni to come out and they stood leaning against one of the boulders, drinking in the cold, fresh air.

Toni said, "My God, Jim. I've never been so scared in my life."

"That makes two of us."

"When I saw you, it was like . . . I don't know, a miracle. I thought they were going to kill me for sure."

"Why? What happened after you left me this morning?"

"I did a stupid thing," she said ruefully. "I thought I could get more information for you on Morley's connection with the bootlegging; I just wanted to help you. I've got a key to the tavern, and while I was rummaging around in Morley's office he showed up to meet Burleigh and caught me. He was pretty ugly; he slapped me around. But I didn't tell him anything. After Burleigh came, they decided to bring me out here. They didn't say much, but I knew they were going to kill me."

"You're lucky they didn't," Flagg said. "We're both lucky to be alive."

She shivered. "What happened in the mine . . . it was awful. The shooting, all those explosions, that man screaming . . ."

"Don't think about it," Flagg told her.

He took her arm and steered her around the boulder, down to the road. Toni stared at the dead man sprawled on the slope, at the dead Doberman at the bottom, but she didn't ask any questions.

They descended the mountain rapidly, staying in the cover of the trees for the most part, stopping now and then to rest. There was no sign of the remaining guard. Either he had cut and run, or he'd gone around to the main entrance to investigate the explosions; he couldn't have missed hearing them where he'd been perched on the flat-topped rock.

An hour later they reached the creek. Flagg went ahead to make sure nobody was hanging around the Falcon pickup. Nobody was. Then he came back and got Toni and took her to the turn-around.

And took both of them and the Falcon away from there.

TWENTY

Churlak said, "Did you have to blow the goddamn place up?"

"It was either that or get blown away myself," Flagg said. He hadn't told Churlak about Toni's being there, about going down like the Lone Ranger to rescue her. It wouldn't have improved his standing with the Organization and he had enough black marks against his record as it was. All he'd said was that he had been spotted and trapped in the tunnel, with the only way out being to use the grenades. "I just didn't have any choice in the matter."

"You're sure the whole still went up?"

"Positive. There won't be much left for the Feds to sift through."

"I liked it better the other way," Churlak said. "The Feds raiding the place, getting all the credit."

"So did I. I wish it could have worked out that way."

"Yeah. It would have made them happy, kept them off our backs for a while. But all right, no use crying over spilt hooch. The still's shut down for good and that's the main thing. You say Morley Ogden's dead?"

"I don't know it for sure," Flagg said, "but it's likely.

I threw the first grenade right near where he was standing."

"Well, Ogden's only a small fry; it doesn't matter if he's dead or not. The good news is that Burleigh wasn't there to get blown up too."

"Why is that good nws?"

"The Feds'll pick him up. That way, they get something out of it—the head of the whole moonshine operation."

"He may implicate Lyons."

"So what? Let them chew on each other. That's what'll happen; neither of them will say a word about the Organization."

Flagg tucked the telephone receiver between his shoulder and chin and loaded his pipe from his pouch of tobacco. He was in his room at the Restful View Motel in Applegate and it was two hours since he and Toni had driven out of the Siskiyou wilderness, taking the long way around, on secondary roads, so they wouldn't have to pass the private road that led up to the mine— just in case anything had been going on there. He had sent Toni out for something to eat and a bottle of bourbon, so he could call Churlak and make his report. The bourbon wasn't for any kind of celebration; there was nothing to celebrate. But he damned well *did* need a drink, as early in the day as it was.

He said to Churlak, "When do you want me back in San Francisco?"

"As soon as possible. When can you get here?"

"Not until tomorrow night, probably."

"Why not sooner?"

"I've got a couple of loose ends to tie off," Flagg said.

"Okay?"

"I guess it'll have to be. But it won't give you much time."

"What do you mean?"

"I've got another job for you," Churlak said. "Up in Washington, this time. A potentially dangerous leak in the gambling setup the Guardino brothers are running for us in Seattle. I want you briefed and on your way by day after tomorrow."

Flagg sighed. "I was hoping for a few days off."

"No chance. Work is all you get for a while. Just so you don't get complacent and screw up again. You understand?"

"I understand," Flagg said.

Churlak signed off and Flagg went over and sat in one of the chairs to smoke his pipe and wait for Toni to come back. He needed a drink more than ever, now. But that wasn't the only reason. He only had a few more hours to himself, before the Organization owned his time again for an indefinite period, and he wanted to make the most of them. Toni had told him while they were driving how grateful she was to him for saving her life. He had an idea she might want to demonstrate her gratitude in one or two interesting ways.

He was right.

She did.

FINE MYSTERY AND SUSPENSE TITLES FROM CARROLL & GRAF

☐ Ambler, Eric/BACKGROUND TO DANGER	$3.95
☐ Ambler, Eric/A COFFIN FOR DIMITRIOS	$3.95
☐ Ambler, Eric/JOURNEY INTO FEAR	$3.95
☐ Brand, Christianna/TOUR DE FORCE	$3.95
☐ Brand, Christianna/DEATH IN HIGH HEELS	$3.95
☐ Brand, Christianna/GREEN FOR DANGER	$3.95
☐ Carr, John Dickson/THE DEMONIACS	$3.95
☐ Carr, John Dickson/THE GHOSTS' HIGH NOON	$3.95
☐ Carr, John Dickson/THE WITCH OF THE LOW TIDE	$3.95
☐ Collins, Michael/WALK A BLACK WIND	$3.95
☐ Fennelly, Tony/THE CLOSET HANGING	$3.50
☐ Gardner, Erle Stanley/DEAD MEN'S LETTERS	$4.50
☐ Gilbert, Michael/OVERDRIVE	$3.95
☐ Graham, Winston/MARNIE	$3.95
☐ Griffiths, John/THE GOOD SPY	$4.95
☐ Hughes, Dorothy B/RIDE THE PINK HORSE	$3.95
☐ Hughes, Dorothy B/THE FALLEN SPARROW	$3.50
☐ Kitchin, C.H.B./DEATH OF HIS UNCLE	$3.95
☐ Kitchin, C.H.B./DEATH OF MY AUNT	$3.50
☐ Pentecost, Hugh/THE CANNIBAL WHO OVERATE	$3.95
☐ Queen, Ellery/THE FINISHING STROKE	$3.95
☐ 'Sapper'/BULLDOG DRUMMOND	$3.50
☐ Stevens, Shane/BY REASON OF INSANITY	$5.95
☐ Symons, Julian/THE BROKEN PENNY	$3.95
☐ Symons, Julian/BOGUE'S FORTUNE	$3.95
☐ Westlake, Donald E./THE MERCENARIES	$3.95

Available from fine bookstores everywhere or use this coupon for ordering.

Carroll & Graf Publishers, Inc., 260 Fifth Avenue, N.Y., N.Y. 10001

Please send me the books I have checked above. I am enclosing $_____ (please add $1.25 per title to cover postage and handling.) Send check or money order—no cash or C.O.D.'s please. N.Y. residents please add 8¼% sales tax.

Mr/Mrs/Ms _____
Address _____
City _____ State/Zip _____
Please allow four to six weeks for delivery.